Glory Days

By D.F. Zaman

Acknowledgements

This book is dedicated to all the people who made my three years as an undergrad, happy years.

Special thanks to Vajihe Golmazari, cover illustrator.

Prologue

Bengal, India, 1954. A fragile-looking little girl of about three stands at the foot of a large double bed, a palong, on which is lying a distinguished looking man of about forty, poring over a broadsheet newspaper.

The child begins to sway slightly while clinging to the palong. She appears unstable on her feet.

"Abba!" she whispers before collapsing onto the polished stone floor with a thud.

Hearing the sound, the man puts the newspaper down and leaps out of bed, seeing the child gasping for breath on the floor.

"Ginny beti breathe! Breathe beti breathe!" he urges the child as he cradles her in his arms while rocking to and fro frantically before yelling, *"Saleha! Sarita! Get in here!"* in his native Bengali.

"Saleha! Get some water! Hurry! Sarita! Call the doctor! Hurry!"

Two slender, doe-eyed girls, dressed in salwar kameez, stand in the doorway, with wide, startled eyes.

They scramble to follow the man's instructions while the man remains sitting on the polished stone floor, rocking back and forth in a frenzy while trying to breathe life back into his dying child.

Chapter One – Boy Meets Girl

A students' union at a university in England. A boy and a girl lock eyes and cannot look away.

Everyone and everything around them fades... into insignificance. They are the only two people in the room, the only two who matter.

Emboldened by the girl's steady, unflinching gaze, the boy ventures forward and inches towards her.

Boldly, he edges forward, closer, closer, ever closer until he is standing just two feet away from her.

"Would you... would you like a drink?" he asks confidently, sure of an affirmative response.

The girl's eyes widen in surprise.

"Er... no thanks."

The boy is staggered. The boy steps back as if he's been punched.

A look of confusion floods his face.

"All this time flirting, all this intense, unflinching eye contact. What just happened? This can't be right!" he thinks to himself.

Taken aback but ever hopeful, he tries again.

"Er... would you... would you like a cigarette?"

This is even worse. This time, the girl crinkles her nose in disgust.

"No, thank you."

The young man is confused. The rejection is so… unexpected.

"I thought I was in there. What just happened?" he berates himself silently, confused.

The boy scratches his head. He takes a step back. He withdraws, ego bruised.

"What just happened? Where did I go wrong? Am I losing my touch?"

Desolation shows on his face.

The girl is unimpressed.

Dejected, the boy slinks away…

Chapter Two

"You Flipping Great Tonka! He was trying to chat you up!"

It happened last night at the students' union. I was just standing there minding my own business when a boy started staring at me for no reason! He stared and stared and stared and stared and he wouldn't stop staring!

I thought to myself, "Has no one ever told you it is rude to stare?"

His eyes were boring through me. It was so intense. It was scary.

At first, I tried looking away to make him stop staring but then, when I turned my head, he was still staring!

I tried to look away again. When I looked back a second time, he was still staring!

I started to get cross. I decided to give as good as I got. I decided to stare right back at him to show him that I wasn't scared. If this was a staring match, I was determined to win! So, I stared right back at him and stared and stared and stared some more!

"That'll show him!"

I was determined to win the staring match.

And then, it happened.

He caved. He gave in. He looked down.

I thought. "Yes! I win! I've won the staring match!"

I was jubilant but only for a second because guess what? Guess what he did next? You'll never believe it! He looked up and started staring again!

I thought, "Oh no! Not again! This is getting really boring now!"

But I was determined to win the staring match. I was not going to give in! I was not going to let this strange boy win!

So, I stared right back at him to show him that he couldn't scare ME by staring. I was determined to give him a dose of his own medicine.

"Rude boy, going round the union staring at innocent people, making them feel uncomfortable," I thought. "I am not going to let him win!"

And then, he did something unexpected.

He smiled. He smiled a real smile that looked genuine that reached right up to his eyes.

I felt terrible. I thought.

" You poor little man! All this time, you were trying to be friendly and I thought you were a prat! You poor little man!"

I felt awful. I felt awful for getting this poor innocent man so wrong. I thought he was trying to intimidate me by staring at me when all the time, he was just trying to be nice. So, I smiled at him to show that there were no hard feelings. I flashed him my most brilliant, my warmest smile.

And then, he did something unexpected. He started coming towards me from the other side of the union! I was only being friendly. I didn't expect him to come over for a chat! He kept moving closer and closer and closer still until he was standing just two feet away from my face. Once he was standing in front of me, this stranger, he started asking me questions and being really nosy!

He said,

"Would you like a drink?"

Well, I'm teetotal so I said,

"No."

Then, he got nosier still. He asked,

"Would you like a cigarette?"

I was horrified so, I said.

"No!"

I was horrified that anyone would think that I would want to smoke! Do I look like someone who wants to empty out her pockets to ruin her health? Do I look like a twerp?

My outrage must have shown on my face because he began to back away but what I couldn't understand was why he looked so upset. Why was he taking it so personally that I don't smoke or drink? What has it got to do with him? Why is it so upsetting to him that I choose to live a sensible life? What right does HE have to tell me how to live my life?

I was left fuming inside. I confided in a boy called Andy in our halls of residence. Andy is two years older than us. He's in his third year. He's doing Engineering while I'm reading English lit. I told him all about the strange boy in the union who goes around staring at innocent people for no reason, making them feel uncomfortable and then, quizzes them ferociously about their lifestyle and judges them if they don't smoke or drink!

I was livid. I expected Andy to be livid too. I expected him to sympathise with me and be angry too but he didn't! I'll tell you what he did say and it was not what I expected at all. He said,

"You flippin' great Tonka! He was trying to chat you up! Poor man. You give him the come-on and then, knock him down flat!"

"Huh?" I thought. "Huh? That was chatting up? He was chatting me up? How was I supposed to know that?" There are no men in my immediate family, just me and my mum and my aunty and her two daughters!

Plus, I had just come out of a girls' school. I've never been a boy. How would I know how it feels to be a boy, how a boy's mind works? The only boys I know are pop stars on my bedroom wall! How would I know what's going on in a boy's mind? No one tells me anything!

Now, that I wasn't in a girls' school and there were boys about, I realised I was going to have to be careful. "No more faux pas where boys are concerned," I told myself. *"I have to ask Emma how their minds work. She's got a brother. She'll know!"*

Little did I know that in my first year at university, I would be the queen of faux pas, a clueless teenage girl from an all-girls' school!

It wouldn't be too long before I'd put my foot in it again!

Chapter Three

"Help! He's Doing Things with His Knees!"

It wasn't really my fault, what happened with Peter. The girls told me I could trust him. They said he was a "really nice guy," so when I invited him back to my student room to see my school barbecue photographs, I couldn't have known what he was going to do!

When I said, "Would you like to come to my room to see my school barbecue photos?"

I meant,

"Would you like to come to my room to see my school barbecue photos?"

It turned out that Peter thought I had meant something else!

I first realised that I had made a mistake when I pulled out my photo album with my school barbecue photos and he showed no interest whatsoever in them at all.

He seemed to be interested in something else!

This boy lounged back on my single bed, one knee pointing North West, the other one pointing South East with his arm behind his head, giving me "*Come hither*," looks all evening!

It was embarrassing.

I didn't know what to do with myself. More to the point, I didn't know where to look!

At one point, I panicked. I decided to pray for help.

I am not kidding! At one point, I started praying quietly to God for help because it was so embarrassing!

I prayed, "God, please make him sit up. I don't know where to look!"

Just as I said that, as if by some miracle, he actually sat up! I felt so LOVED. I thought it was a miracle! I really did! I could imagine a Hallelujah chorus with the music swelling up to a crescendo, going,

"Hallelujah! Hallelujah! Hallelujah! Halle..eh..lu..jah!"

But it only lasted a minute because, after about a minute, he flopped down and started giving me "Come hither," looks again!

The Hallelujah chorus choked.

I began to get desperate at this point.

I was thinking, "My God! My God! Why hast thou forsaken ME? LOOK! He's doing things with his knees!"

I felt so abandoned by God. I thought,

"I'm a nice person. I give to charity. I do voluntary work. I help my mother. WHY.... why God why have you done this to me?"

It was obvious that he was trying to draw attention to a certain part of his anatomy and he kept staring at me just like the other guy in the union so I decided desperate measures were needed to get his mind off whatever it was on so I thought I'd distract him by talking really fast .... about Australian soaps!

You see, whenever I get nervous, I talk really fast. I ramble. It's a sign of nerves so I went on and *on and on about Aussie soaps because I was nervous and I didn't know what to do.*

"Do you like Neighbours? I love Neighbours, you know the Aussie soap with Scott and Charlene and Mike and Jane? Didn't you think it was brilliant when Charlene gave Jane a makeover and she looked a million dollars and Mike asked her out to the dance? Oh, I just LOVED that episode! Didn't you?"

And then, before he had a chance to get a word in edgeways, I went on...

"Don't you think Scott and Charlene make a lovely couple? Didn't you think it was funny when he found out in the wedding ceremony that her middle name was Edna, a granny name? That was so funny. I love Neighbours!

Home and Away is good as well. Kylie's sister, Danni was in that. I love Home and Away as well. That lot sing the theme tune together sometimes on Friday nights when they watch it together before they hit the union."

This embarrassing boy was making me nervous, giving me funny looks and behaving so strangely that I just kept on talking and talking and talking to try and stop him from saying something I didn't want to hear, to try and take his mind off whatever it was on. It was horrible.

So, I rattled on and on for what felt like hours and when he finally got up to leave, I felt a flood of relief!

I had managed to studiously avoid looking down while rabbiting for what felt like an age.

"Well, I'll be off then," he said finally as he got up to leave.

I was thinking, "Finally! Finally! Oh, thank God!"

But outwardly, I said brightly, a little too brightly,

"Oh, all right then! Take care. See ya! Bye!"

"Why do boys have to behave like berks?" I wondered. "If he'd just been normal like my female friends, Emma and Chrissie, I would have been fine. We might have become friends. Why did he have to behave like that? Why couldn't

he behave like a normal person like Christine? She never does things with her knees! I invite HER back to my room all the time! I never have any problems with HER!"

I decided never to invite a boy back to my room again no matter how nice he seemed and no matter how many girls said that I could trust him.

He had shown no interest whatsoever in my school barbecue photos from my last days at sixth form. I was insulted. He was so rude, lounging there constantly trying to draw attention to his bits! It was embarrassing! I was outraged.

The next day, I complained to Emma, my Titian-haired next-door neighbour who lived in the student room next to me.

I poured out the whole sordid story about Crotch-man's antics and I expected her to be outraged as well...but she wasn't. She wasn't surprised at all.

I was stunned.

"Emma, you don't seem a bit surprised. Why? Why aren't you surprised? Am I missing something?"

Emma tut tutted and shook her head before replying,

"Well, of course, he's going to do that Danikins if you invite him back to your room. It's like inviting someone back to see your etchings!"

"What etchings?" I asked, confused. I had no idea what she was talking about.

"If you invite a boy back to your room, he's going to get the wrong idea."

"Why? Why should he get the wrong idea? I invite Chrissie back all the time and SHE never gets the wrong idea! She never does things with her knees! I never have any trouble with HER!"

Emma sighed and looked at me kindly.

"Danita, that's because she's a girl. He did what he did because he's a boy!"

"But that's so SEXIST! He did all that just because he's a BOY! What happened to equality? I thought we were all equal now. It's 1990 for heaven's sake!"

"Well, some things never change Danikins."

"Well, I made sure he'll never come back again, not after the way I talked nineteen to the dozen and didn't let him get a word in edgeways. I'm sure he got the message. He's NEVER coming back again!"

Chapter Four- Emma To The Rescue!

I was WRONG! He did come back! A week after the first traumatic encounter, he was back! I realised my *"talk his ear off so he never comes back,"* technique hadn't worked when I saw his tall, lean figure loping towards me as I was walking back to my room in my halls of residence from the communal kitchen.

"Oh no! Not again!" I thought to myself, my heart sinking.

I thought I had made it clear to Crotch-man that I wasn't interested and yet, here he was again!

"What am I going to do? What am I going to do? I can't go through hours of him giving me "Come hither looks" and doing funny things with his knees again!" I thought to myself in a panic.

"Hi," he says as he looms over me, a smug smile on his face.

"I thought I'd come over and see you again. I won't take much of your time. I'm only going to be five minutes."

Five minutes? FIVE minutes! I didn't want to give him five seconds after what he'd put me through the last time, trying to draw attention to his bits!

Once we were in my room, I panicked. I couldn't bear the thought of going through what I went through the last time. I had to get him to leave somehow.

So, just as he sat down, I said,

"Oh, my goodness! Is that... Emma?"

I made out that there was someone knocking at my door!

There was no knocking! I was just was desperate to get him to LEAVE, this man with all the sophistication and subtleness of a horny cave dweller!

"Hold on! Let me go and find out if it's Emma at the door!" I said, desperate to get away.

I dashed out of my room and knocked frantically on Emma's door.

"Please God, let her be in," I prayed silently. "Please Emma. You have to be in!"

I was so relieved when the door opened and Emma poked her head around the door.

"Em...oh thank God you're in! I need you. He's back! He's back again!"

"Calm down Danikins. Who? Who's back again?"

"HIM! The man with the crotch! He's back again. I need you to help me to get rid of him Em... PLEASE?"

Emma sighed. She shook her head wisely. She smiled.

"All right Danikins. I'm coming. Emma's coming to the rescue!"

In the background, I could see Emma's boyfriend chuckling heartily. I gave him a friendly wave. He was not to blame for how another boy was behaving. He's not responsible for his entire sex! I think he found it funny to see how the other half live!

"Right, don't worry Danita. We'll get rid of him." Emma reassured me as she stepped out of her room and headed for mine.

"Thanks, Em. I owe you. I really owe you," I responded full of gratitude, relieved that she was there.

My mother used to say, "A friend in need is a friend indeed."

Emma, I decided at that moment, was a true friend.

Calmly, she strode into my room and once she was in the room she began to fret. Her beautiful smile was quickly replaced with a worrying frown. She looked at me sternly, and in a stern, authoritative tone, she asked me,

"Danita, have you started your essay yet?"

I was shocked. I thought to myself,

"Essay? What essay? I haven't got an essay to do this weekend? What is she talking about?"

"Your ESSAY Danita. Your ESSAY!"

Emma was looking at me intensely, her eyes very, very wide. She was giving me the strangest look.

I looked back at her confused for a second and then, the penny dropped!

"OH! My ESSAY!" I replied. "I remember. YES! My ESSAY! I have to do my.... ESSAY!"

"Have you started it yet?" asked Emma with the strange look still in her eye.

"Er..no. I haven't."

"WHEN do you have to get it in by?"

"Er... tomorrow morning at 9 o'clock."

"Danita Khan! You are a shocker! An essay deadline for 9am tomorrow and you haven't even started working on your essay!"

"No, no. I haven't even done the secondary reading yet!"

"SHOCKING! You have got to get to work RIGHT NOW!"

"I know," I replied. "I have to get to work RIGHTAWAY! I haven't even got five minutes!"

I turned my gaze to Peter, hoping he would take the hint.

Luckily, the boy got the message. He turned bright red.

"Er...um. I'll be going then," he said, looking kind of dejected.

"YES! All right then," I said brightly, a little too brightly. He was getting no objection from me!

Emma and I looked at each other and grinned. It had worked. Emma's idea had worked. Girl power!

But as he loped away down the corridor of my hall of residence, this misguided boy, his shoulders slumping, looking dejected, I felt a sudden rush of pity for this silly boy with the awful seduction technique that had left me, horrified.

In spite of the rush of pity, I held back from going after him or showing any sympathy lest I was accused of sending out mixed messages or playing games. I couldn't let pity into my heart, not after the way that HE had behaved!

Chapter Five- Craig

Well, I'm finally here! For the first time, Nan was proud of me. I finally did something right in her eyes, her good-for - nothing grandson who had embarrassed her in front of the entire church and let her down time after time. Finally, I've done something to make my nan proud.

"The first graduate in the family," she'd whispered reverently while holding my university acceptance letter in her trembling hands.

Not bad for the kid who was dumped on his gran for life by his teenage mother who got herself up the duff at seventeen!

By the time Mum had grown up and got herself together, her man didn't want me. He didn't want another man's kid and I preferred to stay with Nan.

Nan's been more like a mum to me anyway than my own mum. My mum's been more like a big sister. It's all a bit messed up.

Nan came down with me on the Sunday to see the place. She had a good look around campus and hung around for a while before my Uncle Dave drove her back home up to Liverpool.

When she said goodbye to me, she hugged me tight and I could see tears glistening in her eyes.

I think she's forgiven me for all the things that I've put her through over the years. My nan's the only person who's ever loved me unconditionally but she's nothing like me. We're chalk and cheese!

My nan's part of the God squad. She believes in things she can't see, in an invisible world that no one can see. She believes in happy endings and fairies, no sorry, angels, not fairies. Then again, what's the difference really? My nan was born at a time when it was normal to believe in things you couldn't see. Me, I need proof before I believe in anything. I don't believe in things I can't see. I prefer to live in reality.

My nan's second home is the church. She loves going on and on about Jesus and about God's love and I think, "God's love? My arse! What about all the starving kids in Africa and all the people who've been abused in the world? I don't think they feel very loved!"

Nan used to drag me to church every Sunday when I was a kid. Then, when I was fourteen, I'd had enough. I rebelled.

The vicar had started to dread seeing me in church because of all the awkward questions I used to ask like the time I put my hand up after a sermon and asked innocently,

"So, Vicar if God so loved the world, then, why did he create the fart?"

You should have seen the vicar's face! I could hear kids giggling in the pew behind me but the vicar wasn't laughing and neither was my nan.

She sat there, her lips in a thin line, looking embarrassed and when we got home, I got a second sermon from her that day!

Even after that, she still insisted on dragging me to church so I decided that drastic measures were needed.

It was Valentine's day, 1985 and I wrote a poem in the Vicar's name and pinned it up in the vestry. It went something like this...

"My wife Angie is a hottie

She has a sexy bottie

I spank it every day

Then, we give thanks to the Lord

And pray."

I named it A Poem for His Wife by Vicar Anthony Levin.

When the vicar realised what I had done, all hell broke loose and I found myself in a whole heap of trouble with my nan!

"Craig! I'm so ashamed of you! I've never been so ashamed of you in my life, making jibes about the poor vicar's wife! How am I going to show my face in church again with a heathen for a grandson? People will be gossiping and saying that I'm not raising you right!" she wailed when she found out what I'd done but the message FINALLY got through to her that day.

She never dragged me to church again.

Chapter Six- A New Adventure

It was a day for celebration when I met up with my friend, Paulami, at Green Park before the two of us left home for the first time to go off to university.

Time hadn't yet broken the bonds of a friendship that had been rudely interrupted when my mother had moved me halfway across town to a new home and a new school. We had been living on a rough council estate called Chalkhill and when the council offered us a new home in a different borough, my mother had jumped at the chance!

I, on the other hand, was not so sure. I had made a lot of friends at my old school. I was settled and I didn't want to move but when you're thirteen, you don't have control. Grown-ups have control. You just have to go along with what they want. I had to leave the school I loved and enrol in a new all-girls school that was the opposite of my old school.

Where my old school had vast playing fields and tennis courts, this school had just a small playground. Where my old school had language labs where we studied French, this new school had none. There was so much talk about poverty and cuts in this part of North London that I had dreams that a teacher had come to my house to ask me to go into space to raise money for the school!

The first week I was there was a shock for me especially when a boy came into the school and a girl went mad.

"Oi! You lot! There's a BOY in the school!"

Angela came running into the hall at break-time, her face flushed from running!

Having just come from a mixed school, I thought

" So what? What's the big deal? They're half of the human race!"

What shocked me was the reaction of the other girls.

"Where? Where?" some of them chorused as they rushed over to the staircase to catch a glimpse of the alien creature, the BOY!

"There it is! There it is!" Angela pointed breathlessly down the stairs to where there was standing a boy of about fourteen with spiky, blond hair.

A group of girls rushed forward to the top of the stairs to see the strange creature, the BOY!

I knew, at that moment, that life was going to be very different at this new school where boys were seen as a rarity, as an exotic species of mammal that was rare!

So, after five years in an all-girls' school, I was going off to university where there were going to be lots of boys, where I was going to have to learn to get on with members of the opposite sex so I felt a bit of research was in order.

It was with this in mind that I had bought a copy of Mizz magazine in which there was an article on the four different types of man and how to get along with them.

There was the Soul Man, the Yuppie and the student and I've forgotten what the last one was.

As soon as Paulami and I had sat down on a clean, dry patch of grass, I whipped out Mizz magazine and we pored over the article to look at what it said about the student male.

"It says you will have to be all earnest and not at all frivolous and you'll have to know when to laugh ironically," I said to my friend. "But how do you laugh ironically? Is it like THIS? Is it like...Huh!"

I tried to do my most scornful laugh. This was a different laugh to the sophisticated laughter I had practised with my friends Deborah and Dinah at school up in the music room when we used to dream of being pop stars!

"Maybe," responded Paulami, apparently un-impressed with my effort at sounding ironic.

"So, how do I know when to laugh ironically? What if I laugh ironically at the wrong time and people get cross with me?"

Paulami shrugged, just as perplexed as I was.

So, this was the backdrop to me starting my course at university. I was a clueless teenage girl from an all-girls' school with no boys or men in my family, an ingénue from an all-girls' school. It was not surprising that I became the Queen of Faux Pas in the first term where men were concerned!

So, that first day when we all nervously peeked out of our hidey holes, our new student rooms, and came out to the shared kitchen to bravely introduce ourselves to our new neighbours, I had no idea what I was doing.

I found myself facing what seemed to me to be a massive male person of about six foot two with eyes of blue who towered above my petite five-foot frame, and when he said,

"Hi! The name's Andy," I was totally flustered and I replied,

"N...no. It's Danita. My name is Danita."

From the look on his face, I realised that I had done something wrong and then, it dawned on me.

"Oh! You mean. YOU'RE Andy! Oh sorry. Nice to meet you, Andy. I'm Danita."

I wish I could say that things got better after that but that would be a lie. They didn't. I'm afraid it was one faux pas after another that first term at university. I never seemed to get it right where boys were concerned like this really skinny, lanky guy called Ron.

The first day I saw him, I thought he was lovely. I had an intuitive feeling that he was sweet and shy and that we were going to be friends. That was until I woke up one morning to the sound of him blasting heavy metal music from his room that he shared with another boy called Moss.

It was like his own personal alarm clock that he used to wake up the entire floor!

I rolled over to my other side, pulled my bedcovers over my head and groaned,

"I want to go HOME!"

Sweet and shy? My FOOT!

Chapter Seven- First Impressions (Craig)

So, Sunday was the night it happened. I met my new partner in crime, Rob!

I had a feeling that we were going to be mates and I was right.

Most of us got here at the weekend, spent most of the weekend getting lost, trying to find our way around campus before finally congregating together as a group in the communal dining room for the first time.

There are sixteen students on our corridor, all sharing a kitchen and three bathrooms and it was only a matter of time before we were going to meet up in the shared communal area to see who we'd be spending the next year with.

Looking around the room, I could see a mixed bunch of eight girls and eight lads as if someone had planned it perfectly in the name of gender equality!

There was this Indian girl with a baby face who stood out because she was so small. I didn't get her name. She's about five feet tall with dark hair and big dark eyes. She looks too childlike like a little doll. Not my type. Not my type at all.

I scanned the room for talent until my gaze rested on a girl who had real potential. Lara is her name, long, lean body, silky, hazel hair right down to her waist with a wiggle in her walk and a giggle in her talk!

I thought there was some serious potential there for the first few weeks. I was getting my hopes up until I realised that she lives in Fantasy Land. She's a Bible basher like my nan. Don't get me wrong. I love my nan but I don't want to date her!

So, if the women in my halls of residence are anything to go by, it seems I'm going to be single for quite a while...

Chapter Eight- Wigglebum

Of all the boys I met on Tuesday night, the least intimidating one was Rob. He is adorable.

Being out of school and at university felt really intimidating at first because everyone is so much bigger than me. They all loom above me, especially the boys.

I'm only five feet tall because of childhood anorexia. I starved myself for two years during my growth period, trying to be perfect and please everyone after someone criticised me for being 7 stone, and the doctor told me that I had stunted my growth. I think the exact words he said when he faced me crossly was,

"Your bones were able to grow these last two years but your pituitary wasn't functioning properly because of the lack of nutrition so you've stunted your growth."

I had gone down from 7 stone to 5 stone and had become skeletal. I cried when he told me that the damage I had done to myself was irreversible. I had lost two years of growth and there was nothing anyone could do about it, nothing that could bring those two years back.

So, I am the little one in the group, the petite one.

It was all very intimidating at first to be around all these people who towered over me but after we sat down at the dining table and got chatting to each other, I began to feel a bit better especially when I exchanged glances with Rob who was sitting opposite me. There was nothing intimidating about the dreamy eyed, smiley faced boy sitting opposite me with the corn-coloured hair.

Then, there was the red-haired girl sitting to my right who I learned was living next door to me. She had a pretty girl-next-door look to her and was very disarming with her warm, unpretentious personality and her open, friendly manner.

But all heads turned when another girl entered the room, the enigmatic Lara! Literally, all heads turned when she sashayed into the room. Long, silky hazel hair that hung to her waist, beautiful, wide, hazel eyes, a perfectly formed heart-shaped face that tapered to a delicate point, a long elegant neck and a figure to die for. Lara was the stunning beauty that made the rest of us, girl-next-door types feel insecure.

"Hi everyone. I'm Lara!" she gushed as she breezed in gaily. "Sorry, I'm late. How is everyone?"

There was a chorus of *"Hello. All right."* in response to her breezy greeting.

To say I was intimidated by her would be an understatement. She seemed so sure of herself even in front of a crowd unlike shy, nervous me.

But, over the following weeks, that initial sense of awe turned into active dislike.

Emma and I decided that we didn't like her. We even had a name for her. We started to call her Wiggle-bum in private because of the way she walked. She kind of swayed from side to side like a supermodel when she walked. I mean who walks like that in real life? We decided it must be a put-on to impress the boys.

Then, there was the day when she said,

"Ooh, I feel faint! I feel as if I'm going to pass out!" just when the boys happened to come along!

You should have seen the concern on Craig's face as he rushed to her side. You could have seen his eyes popping out when he said,

"Don't worry Lara. I'll save you. I'll carry you back to your room!"

"Ooh Craig. You're my hero. You're so strong!"

Emma and I looked at each other. We were trying not to gag.

That was the day that Emma and I decided to call her Wiggle-bum.

"God, she is so fake," Emma said after that. "You can see she's one for the boys."

"Ooh save me fellas! She thinks she's Penelope Pitstop!" I chipped in.

"I can just imagine Craig saying, "Ooh Lara, bend over please so I can get a tan because I know the sun shines out of your backside!" Emma added, a mischievous grin on her face.

We both burst out laughing at that one!

In the first few weeks of meeting the beautiful Lara, I had written her off as "one for the boys," the kind of girl who was an attention-seeker who liked to have the boys fawning all over her, the kind of girl who saw other girls as rivals, as competition.

She was definitely NOT one of us... or so I thought... at the time.

Then, just when I had written Lara off as a shallow attention seeker, a bottom wiggler who was not worthy of my time, something happened that took me completely by surprise.

I had just got off the phone from talking to my mum. It had been a few weeks since she had left me at the university and had humiliated me by asking the hall warden, Parminder, to look after me as if I were a little girl!

My mother had scolded me on the phone for not calling her every day.

"So, you've forgotten your mother now that you're at university and having fun with your new friends. You've forgotten your single parent mother who raised you alone without a penny from your father."

"Mother, I've been really busy, getting used to a new place. I've been phoning you every Sunday. It's not like I don't bother to call."

My mother sniffed on the phone.

"All I'm saying is- don't be selfish like your father. He never thought about anyone but himself. I had to sacrifice my whole life to do the mother's job, the father's job, everything alone."

I sighed and shook my head.

I heard this so many times, my mother's sacrifice, never marrying again in case a new man hated me, another man's kid, never having more kids in case I felt less loved.

"Amma, I haven't forgotten you. I haven't forgotten all the things you've done for me, the sacrifices you made. I'm just in a new place, finding my feet. I do call you once a week!"

By the time I got off the phone, I was nearly crying. I had always tried to be the perfect child to make up for my mother's suffering and her sacrifice, to make up for the wrong that he had done to her but no matter how much I tried to be the perfect child, I never felt as if anything I did was ever going to be enough. I needed to be able to breathe and to be just like any other teenager and not to have to spend my whole life making up for the sins of my absent father!

My inner turmoil must have shown on my face because when I returned to my halls of residence, Lara appeared just as I was going back to my student room and she enquired in the softest voice,

"Danita, are you all right?"

I opened my mouth to say the usual,

"Yes, I'm fine. Thank you."

But I couldn't. I burst into tears.

"Oh Danita, I'm so sorry. Whatever is the matter? You look as if you need a friend. Why don't you come back to my room and we can talk about it? You look as if you really need a friend right now."

Surprised by her sensitivity and genuine concern, I nodded, furiously blinking back tears as she ushered me into her room.

"She plumped up some cushions on an armchair and said,

"Here, sit here. Sit yourself down."

And as I lowered myself down into the soft plush chair, she started rubbing my back gently to calm me down as she knelt beside me, her eyes wide with concern before handing me a tissue to wipe away my tears.

And that's when I saw it, the poster in her room. I couldn't believe it. This girl, Lara, who I had written off as a shallow flirt who only cared about being the centre of attention was not so shallow after all!

The poster on her wall was called "*Footsteps in the Sand*" and it was a picture of a sandy desert with footsteps in the sand and on the poster, it said,

"One night, a man had a dream. He dreamed that

he was walking along the beach with God.

Across the sky flashed scenes from his life.

For each scene, he noticed two sets of

Footprints in the sand; one belonging

To him and the other to the Lord."

When the last scene of his life

Flashed before him

He looked back at the footprints in the sand

He noticed that many times along the path of

His life, there was only one set of footprints

He also noticed that it happened at the very

Lowest and saddest times of his life.

This really bothered him and he

Questioned God about it.

"Lord, you said that once I decided to follow

You, you would walk with me all the way

But I've noticed that during the most

Troublesome times of my life

There was only one set of footprints

I don't understand why when

I needed you most, you would leave me."

The Lord replied:

"My precious child,

I love you and I would never leave you

During your time of trial and suffering

When you see only one set of footprints

It was then that I carried you."

I was stunned.

This girl who I had written off as a flibbertigibbet was just like me. She was deep. She pondered the meaning of life, her reason for living, the reason for her existence, the meaning of life!

She was so much more than I had given her credit for. She wasn't just some shallow twerp who was all about flirting and attention seeking just because she had child-bearing hips and consequently, wiggled when she walked!

She had a soul, a heart, a mind that thought about deeper things and she believed in a higher power, a divine force that was behind the creation of the world. She was like me!

I had been wrong about Lara, so wrong. I felt terrible about objectifying another woman just because of her looks. I felt like Lizzie Bennett in Jane Austen's Pride and Prejudice, chastened when she realised that she had got Mr Darcy wrong, oh so wrong.

That was the day that Lara stopped being Wiggle-bum and in the weeks that followed, she became a friend.

Chapter Nine- Working Class Hero

While I was making new friendships with girls like Lara, Chrissie and Emma, I was shy with the boys.

I noticed Rob though even on the first day when he sat next to me at the kitchen table, looking equally sensitive and shy.

"Thank God! I'm not the only one," I thought as we exchanged tentative smiles.

Rob looks sensitive with his wide, translucent, forget-me-not blue eyes. He looks like a dreamer lost in the furthest reaches of his imagination, somewhere only he can go.

His corn-coloured hair is often ruffled and sticking up slightly with a hint of the "just got out of bed," rumpled look. He has the air of someone who needs looking after who brings out the protective, maternal side in girls.

He's the exact opposite of his friend Craig with his high cheekbones, his sharp, darting, piercing eyes and his slightly pointed chin. Rob's face still has a hint of baby-fat which gives him a baby face compared to the more angular Rob.

You'd never put Rob and Craig together. They're exact opposites. Where Craig is spiky and sharp, Rob is soft and dreamy. Where Craig is snappish, Rob is sweet.

Just last Wednesday, I woke up to someone banging on the bathroom door just outside my room in the corridor.

"Rob, are you alive? Some of us need to use the lavvy! Come out of there! Rob!"

More banging.

Andy emerged from his room, yawning, still in his dressing gown, rubbing his eyes, still groggy from sleep,

"What's going on?" he enquired with a yawn followed by a stretch.

"He's making Oscar acceptance speeches on the lavvy in between farts, the divvy! He's been in there for ages. I thought someone had died in there! Rob! Get out you divvy! Some of us need to take a dump! Get out!"

Nervously, I opened my door and peered around it to take in the drama that was taking place just in time to see Rob emerge, looking embarrassed from the shared bathroom and shuffle back to his room.

"Sorry mate! But when a boy's gotta go, he's gotta go!" said Craig, as he rushed into the bathroom and slammed the door.

Later, when I was dressed and leaving the halls of residence for the English Department, having had my toast and tea, Rob and Craig came into the dining room with freshly made toast on wide white ceramic plates.

"Sorry about this morning mate," Rob said apologetically, "but a man's gotta have his dreams, you know."

"Yeah but not on the lavvy in the morning, you dozy dollop!" Craig snapped back. "What was that speech you were making in the lavvy about- I'd like to thank me mother and me brother for believing in me. I'd like to thank me nan".... on the lavvy! Save it for the Oscars mate, the REAL Oscars, not the one in yer head when you're sitting in the lavvy of a morning, taking a dump!"

I sighed as I left without a word. *"That Craig, he's so mean,"* I thought to myself as I rushed out of the door for the first seminar of the day.

Later that day, as I was walking past Rob's door, I was stunned to see a sanitary disposal bag stuck to Rob's door and on it, he had written, *"Sick Bag!"*

Shocked, I knocked on Emma's door.

"Hold on!" she called out before opening her door. Emma's curly russet locks tumbled around her shoulders and her blue-grey eyes lit up with a smile when they met mine.

"What is it Danikins? What's the matter? Come in! You look like you need a friend!"

"Emma, have you seen that sanitary disposal bag on Rob's door? I thought he was so sweet but it turns out he hates women! He's labelled it a sick bag as if he thinks that women are sick or something!"

I expected Emma to look shocked as I had done when I had told her about Peter and his shenanigans but yet again, she wasn't shocked. She wasn't shocked at all. She smiled serenely as she said,

"It's not Rob's fault. It's that Craig. He pinned that up on Rob's door."

"Oh Craig. I should have known! What for? Why's he picking on Rob now?"

"That's just Craig. That's just his sense of humour. He likes to take the mickey out of people, especially Rob."

"But why? Why would he do THAT? Why would he put a women's sanitary disposal bag up on Rob's door and label it a sick bag?"

Emma chuckled slightly as she leaned forward and said conspiratorially,

"Well, there's a story behind that. Apparently, Rob went up to the other boys and said, "Eh, you lot! Have you seen all the sick bags in the toilets?" He thought that all the sanitary disposal bags for women were sick bags."

"What? Even with the drawing of the lady on them?"

"Yep. Apparently, Rob's a bit of an innocent. He doesn't know much about girls. No sisters. Went to an all-boys' school."

"Oh bless," I said sympathetically, a rush of affection sweeping over me for this poor, innocent boy who I had momentarily got so wrong. "Bless his little heart. It's all that Craig's fault. That's so mean. He was shouting at Rob this morning for taking time in the loo. Do you think he hates him or something? Do you think there's trouble brewing between the two of them?"

Emma shrugged nonchalantly, "Who knows? I don't think so. I guess we'll find out though... soon enough."

I shook my head gravely, my heart full of concern for the doe eyed dreamer Rob, being picked on by the sharp eyed, sharp-tongued, hard-faced Craig.

Why did he have to be so mean? He seemed to have taken a dislike to the innocent Rob and was being cruel to him, or so, I thought at the time.

Later on, that evening, I found out I was wrong.

I first heard the sound of the acoustic guitar playing as I trod softly past Craig's room in my pink fluffy slippers on my way to the loo in the corridor just outside Craig's room.

Strains of music wafted on the air and travelled out into the corridor from his room as Craig's door was slightly ajar, and guess who should be sitting on the floor hugging his knees to his chest and swaying slightly from side to side as Craig sat on his bed, strumming his guitar and singing:

"A working-class hero is

Something to be

They keep you doped up with religion

And sex and TV

And you think you're so clever

Classless and free

But you're still f...ing peasants

As far as I can see

A working-class hero is something to be."

And as Craig sang, Rob was looking up at him adoringly as if Craig were the fifth Beatle or something.

"I just don't get boys," I grumbled under my breath.

After a fight like this morning's, a lot of girls would be getting sensitive and giving each other the silent treatment but not these two. Not only were there no hard feelings between these two boys. They were on their way to becoming best friends!

Chapter Ten- Friday Night "Piss-Up!"

Over the following weeks, the sharp-tongued, acerbic Craig took the doe eyed dreamer, Rob, under his wing and the two became fast friends. In fact, the two were becoming a hilarious double act who delighted in entertaining us all.

It wasn't just serious songs like Working Class Hero they sang, these two were like a comedy duo. A few weeks later, as I walked past Rob's room, I caught a glimpse of the two boys singing along to a tampon ad on TV while swaying exaggeratedly from side to side!

"Ooh ooh, ooh ooh, take everything in your stride!" they sang with silly grins on their faces.

What was Craig doing, trying to educate the clueless Rob about women and girls and all things menstrual? First, it was the "sick" bags and now, this!

Tampon ads weren't where it ended either. Over the following weeks, Rob's room started to become a bit of a social hub for all of us, students on the same corridor.

Everyone gravitated towards the wide-eyed, loveable dreamer with his acoustic guitar. With his sweet, sensitive nature, he drew us all in like a magnet.

So, one Friday evening, after I noticed the other students going into Rob's room, I decided to pluck up the courage to knock on his door to see what was going on.

A whole lot of boys and girls were sitting on Rob's bed, all facing the telly and swaying from side to side while singing the theme tune from Home and Away, the Australian soap opera that had become a favourite following the other Aussie soap, Neighbours.

"You know we belong together

You and I forever and ever

No matter where you are

You're my guiding star."

Emma was in there with Andy, the really tall Engineering student with the broad shoulders, and some others like Clare and Cath who I didn't really know very well yet.

"Dani! Over here!"

Emma patted a space beside her on the bed and beckoned me over with a smile.

Over the weeks that followed it became a bit of a ritual on Friday nights before we all traipsed along to the union for my friends to have their Friday night "piss up" before they hit the dance floor!

One Friday, I was flummoxed when I knocked on the door and the other kids chorused,

"Come in Danita!"

"Huh? How do they know it's me?" I wondered. "I'm on the other side of the door!"

A thought entered my mind about my friends who had hitherto seemed so normal.

"Are they psychic or something? Is it like a superpower or something? How do they know it's me from the other side of the door?"

I eyed them all with fascination that evening, wondering what esoteric secrets they knew under that very normal exterior.

I was fascinated by them even when they all got tipsy, playing drinking games to Home and Away.

"Hey, Rob! Let's play a drinking game." That was Craig.

"Let's all pick a character and when our character talks, we take a swig. Whaddya think?"

"I'm in!" replied a grinning Rob.

"Me too!" chorused Andy and the others.

And before I knew it, my fascinating new friends were all getting tipsy around me!

I'm not allowed to drink. I made my mother a solemn vow before she let me go to university that I wouldn't drink or have a boyfriend and so I sat and watched my friends drink around me and transform into people so different from the sensible, sober people they normally are.

At one point in the evening, I found Lara, the normally beautiful, elegant and poised Lara with a saucepan on her head, sitting under the sink in the kitchen and with her was an inebriated Craig, also with a saucepan on his head!

"Hey, Lara! Guess what?"

"What Craig? What?" hiccoughed Lara.

Craig leaned very solemnly towards Lara as if about to share a classified secret. He wobbled slightly before touching her arm lightly and pontificating ponderously,

"If Robin was a bell, we could ring him!"

At this, my two inebriated friends burst into peals of laughter as if he had just made the most hilarious joke in the world!

As they did this, I stood there desperately trying to figure out what was so funny!

Another lad, Malc had wound lots of white loo roll around him and sat at the dining table in the communal dining room, looking like an Egyptian mummy.

He was sitting there, saying to Emma,

"I'll be your mummy! I'm a mummy!"

And that wasn't all. On the other side of the corridor splashing fully clothed in a bath full of water was a happy, smiling girl called Cheryl who was best friends with Lara.

So, Lara was under the sink with a saucepan on her head while her best friend was sloshing around fully clothed in a bath full of water!

Every Friday night, I watched my sane, sober, intelligent friends get wrecked and wake up the next morning with a splitting headache and I struggled to understand why.

"Thank God I don't drive," I thought to myself, "Or I'd have to spend Friday nights ferrying this lot around," after their weekly ritual of getting drunk to relax and unwind after a busy week of seminars and lectures, a ritual they called the "Friday Night Piss-up!"

Chapter Eleven- The Great Jelly Fight

After the initial awkwardness of the first few weeks living together in our hall of residence, people began to bond with one another.

I bonded with Emma and Lara, and Rob bonded with his new bestie, Craig. As we spent more and more time together in the communal dining area in the evenings, we all began to come together as a group.

There was a distinct difference between English literature students like me, Emma and Lara and students like Andy who was an engineer. It was never more apparent than the evening when Emma, Lara and I found the need to wax lyrical over a sunset that we were viewing through the toughened glass windows of the dining room.

"Oh my God! Look at that sunset!" Lara exclaimed, admiring the beautiful mix of colours in the twilight sky, dark blue mingled with marigold and gold in the canopy that was the evening sky.

"It's incandescent!" Lara cried.

"It's translucent!" Emma added.

"It's luminescent," I chimed in.

"It's iridescent!" Emma exclaimed.

"It's transcendent!" Lara proclaimed.

In the kitchen next to the dining room, Lara spotted Andy putting something in the oven and she called out,

"Andy! Get in here! Come and have a look at this sunset!"

Andy, the engineering student, ambled into the communal dining room, tea towel in hand, and as his eyes rested on the flaming sunset that lit up the horizon, he thoughtfully nodded his approval.

"Yeah, it's orange!"

At this point, Emma and Lara fell about laughing while a puzzled looking Andy ambled back to the kitchen.

The first term of the first year was a learning curve like when I learned that it was NOT a good idea to leave essay writing to the last minute and to try and read all of Shakespeare's sonnets in ONE night while pulling an all-nighter!

I also learned not to leave my diary lying around after Rob and Craig got hold of it and humiliated me by reading out loud from it to the whole group in the communal dining room.

I had written about this boy I had a crush on in my seminar and Craig had snatched my diary out of my hand. I ran after him, leaping up again and again, trying to get my diary back as he held it aloft in the air. I was shrieking,

"Give it back! Give it back!"

Craig just chuckled and read *"J'aime Daniel!"* out to the entire common room! I was mortified especially because there was a Daniel in my halls of residence who started giving me coy looks at this point as if he thought I was madly in love with him!

I wish I could say I handled the situation with calm, cool sophistication and with grace but I didn't. I panicked. I got hysterical. I fled to my room, wailing,

"It's another Daniel! It's another Daniel!"

to peals of laughter emanating from the Common Room!

I understood at this point why my cousin in Bengal kept her diary under lock and key with three older brothers in the house. I realised that boys could be nosy!

Apart from that, the first few weeks of our first term at university were filled with attending lectures and seminars, getting to know new people, finding our way around the massive campus and working on our first undergraduate essays.

And before we knew it, the first ten weeks of the first year had whizzed by and it was time for the Christmas party before we all went home for the Christmas break.

And that was when it happened, the Great Jelly Fight of 1989.

It had all begun so well. We had all started off posing for pictures to show the folks back home. Emma and I were sitting on the floor with Rob and Craig with Andy, Lara, and several others kneeling or standing behind us.

The photo session was followed by the Christmas meal. Emma, Lara and some of the others had festooned the dining room with Christmas decorations. Intricately cut paper snowflakes hung from the ceiling and brightly coloured paper decorations of yellow, red and green tissue paper swayed gently above our heads which were adorned with party hats.

Once the main meal was over, out came the mince pies, Christmas cake and a giant strawberry jelly trifle with fruit filled jelly and custard, topped with whipped cream.

Later that night, after I had gone to bed and the friends had got a few drinks in and spirits were high, Emma told me that there had been a jelly fight.

No one knows who threw the first spoonful of jelly but it wasn't long before a war broke out in which the weapon of choice was strawberry jelly.

There was jelly on faces, jelly in hair, jelly on the walls and jelly on the ceiling. Ruby-red globs of jelly ended up splattered everywhere.

No one knows whether it was a coincidence that the warden turned up or whether someone had blown the whistle and brought her down deliberately.

Parminder was a stern-looking, mature student of about twenty-five. She was doing a PhD and funding herself by working as a hall warden, keeping a watchful eye on eighteen and nineteen-year-olds while she was doing her degree and this evening, her watchful eye was very firmly on us, on my group of friends.

"What's going on here? Who made this mess?" she enquired, staring disapprovingly at the ruby-red blobs of jelly that stained the ceiling and the walls.

Most of the students were like frightened kittens at this point, faced with the wrath of the warden, and not a peep could be heard out of anyone.

That was when Andy stepped in to the room like an all-conquering hero just as the warden was sternly surveying the room. He'd popped out to the loo from the rowdy celebrations and had returned to a subdued common room and a stern, disapproving warden, surveying the scene.

"Hi! I'm Andy," he said, extending his hand to Parminder as he strode into the Common Room.

Andy Oakes was a strapping six foot two and having taken a couple of years out after school to volunteer abroad he had started his course at university at the ripe old age of twenty.

So, even though he was a first-year student like the rest of us, he had the air of someone much more polished and mature than those of us who had just come into university in our teens, straight out of school.

Parminder relaxed a little when she saw Andy striding over confidently and when she shook his hand, she smiled as if relieved that another grown-up was in the room.

"Can you tell me what has been going on here please? Someone has made a mess of the common room and none of the students seem to be very forthcoming about WHO is responsible."

"I am so sorry. I had no idea that there had been a jelly fight at all," lied Andy. "I have no idea who could have made such a mess. I have been packing in my room."

"Are... are you sure you didn't see anything?" Parminder persisted, determined to press further.

But a smooth and self-assured Andy replied,

"Positive. I know nothing about what happened here. I saw nothing. As I said, I've been in my room, packing."

Parminder sighed. Andy was so smooth and self-assured. He came across as sensible and responsible, very grown-up, not the kind of irresponsible, immature adolescent who would fling jelly at the walls.

"All right. You may go," she gestured to Andy.

"Thank you. Sorry, I couldn't be of more help," he replied as he turned his back to her and to the rest of the group to return to his room.

And that was when it happened.

There was a collective, sharp intake of breath as Andy turned around and a strange, oppressive tension filled the air. Half a dozen freshers held their breath, desperately hoping that Parminder wouldn't look down because there on Andrew's bottom was incriminating evidence that linked him inextricably to the crime of jelly fighting!

There on the seat of Andy's pants was a massive blob of strawberry jelly!

The group's collective prayers were ignored apparently because Parminder who had been hitherto impressed by Andy's mature and debonair manner DID look down and when she did, her mouth dropped open and her eyes widened in disbelief as she took in the incriminating evidence on the seat of Andy's trousers!

"Andrew, can you come back here please?" she said with a stony look on her face and a steely edge to her tone.

Chapter Twelve- Home for Christmas

Emma wrote to me over the break to tell me that there had been fines! All the students involved in the Great Jelly Fight of 1989 had been rounded up, sent for a stern telling-off to Senate House and fined for their crimes against the environment.

Meanwhile, I was back at home for the Christmas break, being nagged again like a child by my mother and catching up with my old friend from school, Jesmin.

Jesmin was a fragile-looking, delicate girl who was fourteen months my junior and who had been in the lower sixth form when I had been in the upper sixth.

Many were the times when she had sneaked up behind me and my friend Maryam and shouted *"Boo!"* in an effort to scare us, only she couldn't scare a fly because her shout was more like a high-pitched squeak. Jesmin had a very high-pitched, girly voice.

"Oh! I'm scared Jes! I'm so scared!" I'd joke while clutching my chest as if terrified and she'd giggle like a schoolgirl which is what she was!

After my first week at university, I had written letters to friends back home about the thrill of being in a new place that was so grown up!

Over the ten weeks that formed the first term, I had forgotten what I had written in that first week but Jesmin wasn't about to let me forget.

She whipped out my letter from her shoulder bag.

"Um... I got your letter, Dani. It was great but I didn't understand this bit, you know the bit where you said,

"I have learned so much in my first week at university and I feel I have finally come to terms with my identity as an individual entity."

I flushed slightly, feeling embarrassed. I decided that honesty was the best policy.

"Er... you weren't supposed to get that Jes because I didn't get it either."

"Then, why did you write it?" asked Jes puzzled, her forehead forming a delicate frown.

"I was trying to sound sophisticated. I was trying to sound profound. Sorry."

"Wally."

I chuckled and she giggled that high-pitched girlish giggle that was so endearing. She decided, at this point, to change the subject.

"OK, so when's the wedding?"

"Wedding? What wedding?" Now, it was my turn to frown. I had no idea what she was talking about!

"You know! That boy you said was THE ONE in your letter, remember? See, here!"

She pointed to the letter again.

I pored over the letter over the part to which she was pointing to see what I had written and I had written,

"Jes, I've been here for four whole days now and I have found THE ONE! You will never believe it! He looks just like an Asian Elvis! He is so CUTE! I just know that he's THE ONE!"

My mind travelled all the way back to the first week of term when I had gone to an Asian Society meeting and met Shabir. I had fallen madly in love with him for about a week and for a whole week I could think of no one else.

Sadly, my infatuation with the Indian Elvis lasted all of about a WEEK! It all came crashing down to a hopeless end at the end of the first week when he said,

"My mum and dad had the happiest marriage and I want the same for my life. My dad went to work and my mum stayed at home and that's what I want, a stay-at home wife, someone who'll stay at home and have babies and take care of the house while I go to work."

Well, when you're thirty and ready to build a nest, that is fine but when you're eighteen and just out of school, that is the last thing a girl wants to hear.

The next day, I was in agony, a kind of mental and emotional agony.

I imagined myself in the future, barefoot in a steam-filled kitchen, peeling potatoes with a huge belly, saying hopelessly,

"It's triplets... THIS TIME!"

At eighteen, before I had even had a chance to live, this picture of premature parenthood, was terrifying.

So, the next day, I was in agony and I was sure that I would never get over it.

I remember Emma had an inscrutable look on her face as I wailed,

"Oh Emma, Emma! I've liked him for a WHOLE week! I can't just get over him in a day!"

But, as fate would have it, I did. I did get over him in a day!

It was like some kind of twenty-four-hour sickness that worked its way out of my system and was gone!

Twenty-four hours was all it took to get over the man I thought I "loved" for a week but in the second term of my first year, I was going to fall for someone who I would struggle to get over for years to come...

Chapter Thirteen – Daniel

His name was Daniel and he looked like a poet. The first day I saw him, I thought,

"You're a poet and I know it!"

Maybe it was those dark Byronic curls that framed his alabaster brow, those piercing eyes that pointed to an anguished soul but there was something about Daniel that made him stand out.

While all others sat up straight to attention in their chairs, Daniel lounged back with a touch of nonchalance in his air as if to say,

"Come on then. Impress me!"

His eyes lit up in seminars when he talked about poetry and like me, he'd lean forwards and gesticulate expressively with his hands as he tried to make a point.

His intensity, his passion for literature resonated with me and when Emma told me he was the Head of the Poetry Society, I knew I had got him right.

"You ARE a poet! I was right!" I thought to myself triumphantly.

So, I decided to write a little poetry of my own... about Daniel!

"Oh, Lara! Lara! He's got poetic and romantic hair!" I gushed one day while we were having coffee in the Arts Building cafeteria.

Lara's response shocked me.

"No Danita. He just needs a haircut!"

It was brutal.

Where I saw a romantic and sensitive poet with Byronic hair reaching to his sensitive shoulders, she saw a scruffy boy in need of a haircut!

No one seemed to understand how I felt about this boy!

I phoned Mrs Harding, a neighbour I had known from the age of two when I had lived in Stockwell. Mrs Harding had been born in 1899. She'd left school at fourteen to work in a factory, the eldest of ten kids. She and Mr Harding had gone courting when she was twenty and had been happily married for five decades but had no kids.

She used to knit me jumpers when I was seven and say she was my English granny.

Before I could tell her about Danny, she launched into a conversation of her own.

"How's yer mum love?"

"My mum. Er...... she's fine."

I've called you to talk about Daniel. I haven't called you to talk about my mum, I thought to myself but still, she went on...

"I'll never forget your mother. I remember seeing this poor foreign girl, sitting in the park with a little girl, looking like she'd got the weight of the world on her shoulders, far away from home. How's yer mum love?"

"She's... she's fine," I assured Mrs Harding.

Before I could venture any further, she said,

"It's all changed around here you know. It's like Liquorice All Sorts around here. It's like Liquorice All Sorts. You've got black going with white, white going with brown, brown going with black. It's like Liquorice All Sorts!"

"Right," I responded, not quite sure what to say.

Then, she continued...

"Have you got a boyfriend?"

"No."

"Do you like someone?"

"Yes."

"Is he white?"

"Yes."

"I think you should wait."

There was a long silence on my side of the phone. I decided not to tell her about Daniel after all.

In her defence, Mrs Harding was born in 1899 when white people married other white people and Liquorice All Sorts was a brand of sweets confined to bags in sweet shops. She was a good woman with a good heart but she was a product of her time and was struggling to cope with the changes that were happening in the world around her.

Then, there was my mother, another older person from another generation who didn't understand.

Unlike some young people, I had no secrets from my mother. Being the only child in a single parent family meant that we only had each other and so the bond between us was strong. It had been just the two of us since I had been in primary school and so my mother had always been at the centre of my world.

I told my mum about Daniel, about his wavy, poetic and romantic hair and his cute, upturned nose. I showed her the poem I had written when inspired by one of his sneezes in a lecture, a poem I had entitled, **The Lady Writes an Ode Upon Her Lover's Nose**.

I had written the poem at a time when we were studying the Courtly Love Tradition at university. We were reading poems about pale knights, loitering by lakes, pining for ladies, La Belle Dame Sans Merci, and so on...

So, I had written an ode of my very own and it went like this...

What's in a sneeze?

That gentle breeze

A nose that blows

Wavy hair that grows

So that when in lectures I see

I can but STOP

And stare

At HE of the wibble-some nose

And poetic, romantic hair!

When I read this poem out to my mother, expecting rapturous applause, I was disappointed. She was NOT impressed!

"You write poems when he sneezes?

What are you going to do if he burps?"

I was indignant.

"Mother, Daniel is a romantic. It is not romantic to burp. Therefore, he does not burp!"

My mother gave me THE LOOK, you know the one that says,

"Did I really give birth to you? Are you really my child or did they give me a Changeling at the hospital?"

"Mum, I think I love him," I said hesitantly.

"Danita, you don't know this boy! Have you ever even spoken to him?"

I shook my head. My mother continued...

"This LOVE that you talk about is a fantasy. It's not reality. Just because he has wavy hair and a nice nose doesn't mean that he is the right boy for you. You know nothing about his personality!"

"Mum, I think he likes me. He keeps looking over at me and sitting around me in lectures. I think the feeling is mutual."

"Danita, do you think that this boy is going to marry you? He wants to have fun with you but he won't marry you. When it comes to marriage, he will marry someone of his own culture and our people won't have you. They will say, "This is a bad girl. She had a boyfriend." You will end up alone. "Do you want to end up alone?"

"No."

"Then, you have to be PRACTICAL and sensible. Forget about this boy and his burps and his sneezes. Focus on your studies. Be a good girl. Work hard and after university, we will think about finding you a nice boy in the faith for you to marry, OK?"

I realised at this point that my hopeless crush was just that, hopeless, something that would have to remain in the realm of fantasy. It was not practical. It would never be a reality.

All I would get out of this crush would be a handful of poems. I was like the lover in Shakespeare's sonnet writing poems to his mistress eye-brow! All I would have of Daniel would be the poems that I wrote about him, about the forbidden fruit, the love that was unattainable and so, I wrote poetry to express the pain of forbidden love.

One night after I had woken up after a dream of Daniel, I tried in vain to get back to sleep to get back into the dream to see him again. He was a person with whom I could live in my dreams I decided. I could never have something real so I wrote the poem **Dreaming**.

I dreamt of you again last night
For the hundredth zillionth time
I dreamt my arms enfolded you
That you were really mine

I looked across a crowded room
And saw you standing there
Saw the soft look in your warm, brown eyes
The soft waves of your hair

And the lights were dim
But my mind was aglow
With thoughts of what might be
Of the love, the heart that could be mine
Of the dream of you and me.

Do star-crossed lovers ever meet
In the heavens up above

Where a million day-dreams
Find a home
And the only god is Love.

And yet again, you reach to me
With eyes that speak devotion
A look that pierces to my heart
And sets my soul in motion.

Oh lover, though I turn away
You feel my
Silent scream

Though we never meet
In cold daylight
You live with me
In my dreams.

Chapter Fourteen- Rag Week

"FREEZE! Nobody move!" bellowed the balaclava-clad man, dressed all in black as he burst through the doors of the lecture hall!

To my horror, the man was holding a rifle!

I was in shock.

"Oh my God! We're all going to die!" was my first thought.

"This man hates students so he's come to kill us!"

"WHERE is Rebecca Wright?" he demanded in a terrifying, angry tone.

"Oh so, he's after just one girl? He's not going to kill us all?" I thought my heart thumping wildly in my chest.

While I was relieved that he wasn't after all of us, I felt pity for this poor girl, Rebecca.

What could she have done that was so bad that someone would burst into the lecture hall to kill her? What could anyone have done at the age of nineteen that would lead to someone hating them this much?

My heart went out to this poor girl, Rebecca. Whoever she was, she didn't deserve to die like this, a teenager!

"Where is Rebecca?" he demanded again and at this point, a slender, delicate-looking girl with an auburn bob, pale skin and freckles and a heart-shaped face, stuck up her hand.

I was surprised by how well she was taking it. This madman had just burst into the seminar with a balaclava and a gun, looking for her and she didn't even seem bothered. In fact, she was smiling as she put up her hand.

I looked at Rebecca with astonished admiration. She was so brave. She was my age, a teenager and yet, here she was, facing death so bravely, smiling in the face of hate, defiant.

As she put her hand up, the scary man in the balaclava strode over to where she was sitting, defiant and unafraid, and once there, he, aggressively, slapped a box of Milk Tray chocolates onto the wooden ledge in front of her on which rested her notes on the lecture.

Having slammed the chocolates aggressively down onto her notes, he yelled,

"And all because the lady loves Milk Tray!"

I must have looked confused because Chrissie, my friend, whispered in my ear,

"It's Rag Week. People play pranks on each other and raise money for charity."

"Oh! Oh my God!" I whispered back, relief flooding over me.

Rag Week, I learned, was a time to be silly and to have fun, to pay people to do silly things to raise money for charity.

Giant gnomes roamed around campus, stalking students, following them everywhere they went, sitting beside them in lectures and following them to the cafeteria, the restaurant and the students' union.

I say giant gnomes but they were actually volunteer students raising money for charity, dressed in gnome costumes, hired by pranksters to embarrass their friends by following them everywhere in outfits that looked ridiculous.

During Rag Week, I realised for the first time in my life that I was having fun! Being a single parent's child living on a budget with a strict, overprotective mother who didn't let me out on my own until I was sixteen, I had never had much fun before except on the odd, occasion at school but here, surrounded by people my own age, all of us young, all of us teenagers with high spirits, life was fun for the first time.

Rag week pranks were followed by water fights in the summer where we all ran around like big kids, spraying each other with water from water guns and turned up to lectures dripping wet!

When we had been little kids in the seventies, we had all begged our parents to take us down to the ice cream van whenever we heard the music, usually Greensleeves, playing from the ice cream van.

Now, at eighteen, in the nineties, we leapt out of our ground floor windows screaming, *"Ice cream!"* before racing down the grassy slope outside our windows to the ice cream van in the car park beyond to get our ice creams. Then, we'd all flop down contentedly on the grass under the summer sun and lose ourselves in strawberry sauce and soft scoop ice cream. It was like being a child again at eighteen!

For the first time in my life, it felt as if I was LIVING and not just coping, existing, enduring and surviving, a single parent's relatively impoverished child whose anxious mother had forced her to sit at home and study to build a better future while all the other kids were outside with friends and having fun.

For the first time in my eighteen years, after a lifetime of wistfully watching other kids having fun from my window, I was allowed to join in and play and be part of the group just when I was on the verge of adulthood!

Who cared if I didn't know how to ride a bicycle or throw a frisbee as I had never been allowed out to play with the kids in my neighbourhood by my anxious, overprotective mother? I finally got to be part of the group!

We made the most of those heady student days because we knew that it would all be coming to an end within a couple of years. We knew that before long, we would have to discard the exuberance of our young years and adopt the mantle of adulthood. We would all have to go out into the adult world to be sensible, responsible grown-ups to pay bills and mortgages and raise the next generation in the never-ending cycle that was life.

But before that day dawned, we were going to enjoy every moment of our extended childhood, our student years, our Halcyon days.

Chapter Fifteen- Pranksters

Living in the same halls of residence, Emma and I formed a strong bond in our first year.

In between attending lectures, seminars, writing essays and revising for exams, we found time to play pranks on other students in our hall of residence!

The first time was in the second term while we were strolling past Rob's door.

"Emma, do you think that Rob's message board looks a bit sad? He never gets any messages. It must be a bit sad to have a message board and to never get any messages."

"Hmm... you know what Danikins? I think you're right."

We looked at each other.

"Emma, are you thinking what I'm thinking?"

"What?"

"Should we leave him a message? Cheer him up."

"I don't see why not."

"What shall we write?"

Emma cocked her head to one side as if thinking deeply.

"Hmmm.... Let me think. What shall we write? What shall we write? Hmmm..."

Later that evening, we watched gleefully as three very confused boys pored over the message in the communal dining room.

"Aunty Ethel? I haven't got an Aunty Ethel or a dog called Willy!" Rob said, a look of confusion on his face.

"Read it out again," said Craig.

Rob sighed and read,

"Dear Rob,

Aunty Ethel called last night while you were out. She said that Willy the dog has run off with Maisie the rabbit. We believe they have eloped and are headed for the South of France. The whole family is in uproar. Come home AT ONCE!

P.S. Aunty Ethel will be calling you tomorrow morning at 5 am to discuss."

"What divvy wrote that then?" That was Craig.

Rob shrugged, still looking perplexed.

Meanwhile, Emma and I were eavesdropping from the kitchen, stifling childish giggles.

Well, I think that went quite well Danikins. Don't you?" asked Emma, looking very pleased with herself.

"Yes, I think so," I agreed amiably.

"We gave the boys something to talk about and Rob finally got a message on his sad, empty message board. We're a right pair of do-gooders Em, you and me! We should go around leaving more messages for people with sad message boards that are empty and neglected. We should make their day, let them know that someone cares enough about them to leave them a message."

Emma nodded in agreement and so it was decided that we would do this again someday. We two do-gooders would take the time to write silly messages on sad message boards that were neglected and empty.

But the next time, we tried to be charitable and leave a quirky message on someone's poor, neglected message board, things went wrong, horribly wrong.

It was a couple of weeks later as we were strolling past a student room in the corridor adjacent to ours in our hall of residence that we spotted it, another sad, forlorn, neglected message board with no messages, not a single one.

Emma with her big heart was full of pity for the poor student with the neglected message board.

"Tut tut! Poor thing. No messages. So neglected. So sad."

She shook her head and sighed and I asked,

"Shall we do something about it Em? Are you thinking what I'm thinking?"

"I think I might be."

"OK. So, then, what shall we write?"

"Hmmm. Let's see. What's her name? It says Mabel here. It says, Leave a message for me if I'm not in. Mabel. We need to keep it short in case someone wants to leave a real message."

"Hmmm...

How about...

My Darling Mabel

I have been in love with you for a very long time. You move me in ways I cannot understand, you gorgeous, admirable, adorable creature. Marry me Mabel and have my babies! I would like you to have my triplets AND my twins." I suggested.

"That's good," approved Emma. "And add... Marry me my darling and let's ride the ocean of love together forever. Lots of love and kisses from your secret admirer."

"Yes, and add a P.S. Say, "I'm a male model in my spare time. Would you like to see my biceps?" I suggested.

Emma giggled like a mischievous schoolgirl as she wrote the silly message but just as she was about to put the pen back that Mabel had left by her message board, the door opened unexpectedly and a little curious face peeked out.

The noise we were making must have been the reason. We had assumed that everyone would be out at lectures in the middle of the day. It didn't occur to us that Mabel would be in her room at this time of the day.

I panicked.

"Emma! RUN!" I yelled over my shoulder as I made a dash for the door.

Emma duly followed me and sprinted for the door as the startled girl watched a pair of full-grown wallies behaving like silly schoolgirls in their first year at university.

Just as Emma got to the door that connected our corridor to Mabel's she did a sudden U-Turn and said *"Her pen! I need to give her back her pen!"*

Then, she ran back to the astonished Mabel, her hair flying, her bangs falling into her eyes, her face, flushed with embarrassment.

"Sorry! Your pen!" she yelled as she handed back the pen to the girl and then sprinted back!

Once safely back on our own corridor, we both stopped for breath.

We were in shock. How were we supposed to know that Mabel would be in her room at midday on a weekday when most people are in lectures and seminars and how were we supposed to know that there were people called Mabel from China?

"God only knows what she thought of us and God only knows the damage we've done to international relations!" panted Emma as she leaned over with her hands on her knees, trying to catch her breath.

"I know. That was so embarrassing," I replied, clutching my side.

"I don't think I want to do this again," said Emma, chastened.

"Me neither," I agreed.

And that was the end of our stint as pranksters. We had learned our lesson.

We never left a silly message on anyone's door again!

Chapter Sixteen- They Talk To God!

"No drinking, no smoking, no boyfriends, no pork. Don't lie. Don't cheat. Don't steal. Don't hurt anyone. That's Islam," my mother told me when I was eleven. That was my mother's version of the religion of Islam in a nutshell.

When she took me back to Bengal in Asia in 1979, she made me attend Quran classes with her friend's daughter, Farzana.

The teacher was an Eastern man who didn't speak English and he kept yelling at me because I couldn't pronounce the guttural Middle Eastern sounds that he wanted me to pronounce from the back of the throat but how could I? I was only eight and I had never lived in the Middle East. I didn't know how to make guttural sounds like him!

"Khor! Khor! Khor!" he kept on yelling after he lost patience with me and my Western pronunciation.

"Cor," I would respond nervously on the verge of tears.

"No! Khor! KHOR!"

"Cor!"

KHORR!"

I hated being yelled at so I begged Farzana,

"Tell him I'm sick Apa. Tell him I'm sick. He keeps yelling at me."

Farzana duly informed the teacher the next lesson that I was ill and he was fine with this until he spotted me skipping rope at the other end of the apartment!

I didn't expect him to get up in the middle of the lesson to go to the lavatory and so he had spotted me skipping in the hallway near the loo.

I froze in horror as his eyes met mine and I knew I was in trouble.

"HEY!" he yelled at me and pointed in the direction of the living room where Farzana and her brother were having their lesson.

Disappointed and dejected, I headed reluctantly to the living room to read from a book with a foreign alphabet to pronounce foreign words I didn't understand. The man was teaching me to sound out words in Arabic without telling me what they meant. I couldn't pronounce the words and as a child who spoke an Indian language at home, I didn't know what they meant so I wasn't engaging with the lessons. I was bored. I had preferred skipping rope to reading the Quran but my mother insisted on me having these lessons where I was taught to read words in Arabic that I did not understand.

The man who yelled *"KHOR!"* at me indignantly was the first of many Quran teachers.

The next teacher was a woman who had been my mother's student back in the sixties before my mother had moved to Britain and had me in the nineteen seventies.

This woman looked up to my mum, her former teacher so she never told me off even when I dozed off in the lessons because I couldn't understand a word of what I was saying!

It was all Arabic to me and I didn't understand Arabic because my mother tongue was Bengali.

For all I knew, I could be saying that there was a man in the moon or I could be saying, *"Hear ye! Hear ye! Thou shalt have pizza for pizza is GOOD!"*

What was the point of teaching me to read the Quran in a language that I didn't understand so that I couldn't even begin to engage with the lessons? They didn't even give me a translation so I could understand what the Quran was saying!

When my mother's former student got pregnant, she stopped teaching me and she was replaced by a new, older lady and I got instant karma because she started dozing off in the lessons! The minute that I would hear her snoring, I'd let my guard down and think it was safe, but then, she'd suddenly wake up with a snort and scold me!

"Eh...no! Do it again! That was wrong!"

I was astounded. I thought, "How do you know what I was saying? You were snoring just a minute ago! How are you doing that? Snoozing and monitoring me at the same time? What are you, an alien or something?"

The last and final Quran teacher was the one who was most terrifying. He picked his nose in lessons and then, he'd run his finger across the page and order me to follow the text by placing my finger on the page where his finger had been.

I balked. I thought, "I don't want to touch the page that was touched by your finger which was up your nostril just five minutes ago!"

So, Quran lessons were never much fun for me because no one ever gave me a translation so that I could engage with the text that was in a language I didn't understand. I didn't know what I was saying!

So, how could I relate to the religion of Islam when the Quran was in a language I didn't understand? I didn't even know what the book was saying!

By contrast, I found myself, drawn to Christianity because I could understand what Christians were saying in their hymns because the Bible was in a language I actually understood.

In addition to the language barrier, in Islam, there was always the threat of punishment, of God's judgement in the way that I was taught about the religion as opposed to the promise of God's love that was taught in the Christian faith, so what was a child going to gravitate towards, the god of punishment or the god of love?

Naturally, I found myself drawn to the religion that told me, a fatherless child, that God was an adopted father to the fatherless and that he loved us. Plus, I knew that both Islam and Christianity taught belief in the same god of Moses and Abraham, that they were sister religions and not enemies, a perspective that my mother held which was why she didn't mind me going to church with my Christian friends, Cheryl and Lara.

"We believe in the same god so you can go to church with your Christian friends," my mother told me, "but remember, Jesus is a prophet of God, a great man of God, not the son of God because God cannot have babies. He is a spirit. He has no physical body and he is a HE so he can't have a baby. OK? We are friends with the Christians. They believe in the same god as us but you are a Muslim. Remember that even if you go with them to church. Don't forget who YOU are."

So, when Lara and Cheryl used to go to church, sometimes I used to tag along. It was peaceful in the little chapel with the beautiful stained-glass windows.

Most of the times when I went to church with my friends, there was the usual church service with the vicar in his smock standing at the front discussing a text from the Bible and applying it to life after hymns had been sung and the congregation had sat down.

But one Sunday was like no other Sunday. The vicar announced,

"Well, I was talking to God this Tuesday and God said to me,

"Tim, he said, I have given you many gifts with which to serve me, with which to serve my church. Never doubt that I love you even when life challenges you for it is through fire that gold is refined."

My jaw dropped as the vicar casually commented on his conversation with God as if it was the most normal thing in the world.

Excited, I tapped Lara's arm gently and asked,

"Lara, did you hear that? The vicar said that God chats with him! I pray to God all the time. He never says anything to me!"

Imagine my surprise when both Lara and Cheryl turned their heads and chorused,

"He talks to us too Danita," as if casually chatting to the Almighty God of the universe was the most natural thing in the world!

That night, I called my mother.

"Mum! Guess what? You know Lara and Cheryl, the two Christian girls I'm friends with?

"Yes?"

"Well, I found out today that they're like Moses! God speaks to them directly like he did with Moses!"

"Who told you that God speaks to them?" my mother asked, suspiciously.

"They did! They're the chosen people of God."

"Who told you that they're the chosen people of God?"

"They did!"

I heard a sharp intake of breath on the other side of the phone and I could just feel my mother rolling her eyes. There was a slight pause before she responded,

"Danita, perhaps, you should focus on your studies instead of going to church so much. I am happy for you to be friends with the Christian girls because they're good girls. They don't have sex outside of marriage and they believe in the same god as us but you need to remember who YOU are."

"But Ma! They're the chosen people of God. God literally talks to them. They literally have chats with him like every day! How come he doesn't chat with us? Is it because we're not chosen?"

"Danita, everyone is chosen by God because there is only one god and he made everyone so he cares about everyone, not just one group of people."

I knew my mother was right. Everyone must matter to God because my religion teaches that there is only ONE god, the god of Abraham, Moses and Yahshua who most people call Jesus. There isn't a black god called Delroy who made black people, a brown god called Sukhvinder who made brown people and a white god called Alistair who made white people!

There is only one god and one god means that he made us all and that we all matter to him regardless of colour.

My mother obviously felt threatened by how impressed I was by the vicar's declaration of his cosy chats with God.

"No more going to church with your Christian friends Danita. It's fine for you to be friends with these people because they are good girls but you can't convert to their religion. You have your own religion. You are Muslim. You need to remember that."

I decided to let the subject drop at this point. There was no point arguing with my mother and causing her stress but that would not be the last time that I ever went to a church...

Chapter Seventeen- Timid Knock

I stopped going to church with Lara and Cheryl for a while after that. Growing up between two religions and two cultures was confusing.

My Hindu friends felt they were right. My Jewish friends knew they were right. My Christian friends were sure that their way was the only way and my mum was convinced that her way was right! While I followed the "no drinking, no smoking, no boyfriends, no pork," rule to keep her happy, I didn't know who to believe.

Growing up with a multiplicity of ideologies and competing belief systems was confusing and it was going to be another two decades before I would work out what I truly believed.

After getting off the phone from my mother, I decided I needed the comfort of being among friends so I trotted off to Rob's room where everyone congregated to watch Home and Away every Friday evening where they'd all sing along to the theme tune and sway,

"You know we belong together

You and I forever and ever

No matter where you are

You're my guiding star."

Rob's door was shut but I knew they would be in there together as this was the normal Friday routine. Everyone congregated together in Rob's room before hitting the union every week.

I knocked on the door and was astonished when they all called out in unison,

"Come in Danita!" from the other side of the door.

I was stunned. First, I found out that two of my friends are like Moses from the Bible and the Quran. They have cosy chats with God and think it's normal and now, this lot has laser vision like Superman and can see right through the door! Or maybe, they're psychic and I just didn't know!

WHAT was going on?

Curiously and a little nervously, I stepped into the room to greet my possibly other-worldly, psychic friends with supernormal superpowers that they had hidden from me until now.

Desperate to satisfy my curiosity as to the source of their superpowers, I decided to take my courage into my hands and to ask them straight out.

"How did you know it was me from the other side of the door?"

Emma's bright eyes fixed on me before her lips curved into a smile and she replied,

"It's your knock Danikins. You've got such a timid little knock."

"Oh," I replied, disappointed, "I thought you were all psychic!"

At this point, Rob and Craig turned to look at me, merriment twinkling in their eyes and my heart sank because I knew what that meant. I was going to be teased. I had said the wrong thing, and I was going to be teased! I was right because the next moment, they gave each other a look before they burst out laughing and made a show of banging their heads in desperation against the wall!

"Rob, you take this wall. I'll take that wall!" said Craig and the two of them, then, proceeded to embarrass me by mock-banging their heads against the wall as if in despair.

These two love teasing people especially those of the female variety like the time they heard Lara and me complimenting each other in the dining room, adjacent to the kitchen where they were making beans on toast.

"Oh, Lara! I love that outfit on you. It really suits you. You look really nice. You're really pretty."

"Aww. Thank you, Danita. I think YOU'RE pretty. That shade of blue really suits you."

"Don't be silly. I'm nothing next to you. I'm not pretty. You are!"

"Are you joking? With your long dark lashes, big brown eyes and that cute little button nose, you are so adorable."

"Well, you're taller and you look like a model whereas I just look like the average girl next door, all of five foot and a quarter inches!"

"Don't be silly Dani. You're really pretty. You have to know that."

"No, I'm not. You are!"

Rob and Craig must have heard us arguing from the kitchen because when they came into the dining room with their plates in their hands, they were smirking and then, the silliness began.

As soon as they sat down, Craig turned to Rob and said in a high-pitched voice,

"Ooh Rob, you're so pretty. You're so cute. I LOVE you!"

And Rob responded by batting his eyelashes and saying in a voice that sounded like Minnie Mouse,

"No, you! You're so pretty Craig. You! Ooh!"

Lara shook her head and rolled her eyes and whispered,

"Boys! You can't live with them. You can't. You just can't. You really can't!"

Later on, Emma's comment about my "timid knock" really haunted me.

"Do I need to be more assertive? "I thought to myself. "Is that how people see me as some kind of timid person?"

I decided I had to be more assertive. I had to work on it. I had to stop being a silly, insecure teenage girl with a high-pitched giggle that the world couldn't take seriously, knocking timidly on doors like a timid schoolgirl!

I had to practise my sophisticated, womanly laughter and knock on doors assertively like a lady. Yes, that had to be my new goal. "Goodbye giggly teenager. Hello sophisticated woman of the world who knocks assertively on doors," and opens doors that lead to success.

Being assertive was my new goal.

Chapter Eighteen

The Wrong Seminar!

My plan to be more assertive backfired horribly. I woke up one Thursday morning and found to my horror that I had overslept and was hopelessly late. My bedside clock had stopped. The battery had run out and the hands on the clock were not moving any more.

I stumbled out of bed, cursing my alarm clock. What was I going to do? How was I going to explain this to Maggie, my seminar tutor?

I would have to be brave I decided. No more Miss Timid Girl. No more timid knocking on doors like an apologetic little schoolgirl!

I was three months away from turning nineteen and now was the time to learn to be a confident, assertive, sophisticated woman of the world!

All the way to the seminar, I was rehearsing in my head what I was going to say,

"Sorry I'm late. My alarm didn't go off this morning. I am really sorry."

I went over it again and again in my head. I would knock boldly on the door, stride in with confidence like the lawyers on the hit TV show, LA Law. No more timid schoolgirl!

That was the plan anyway. Here is what actually happened...

I did knock boldly on the door to be fair. I strode in fairly "confidently" to a sea of unfamiliar faces.

Boldly, I carried on...

"Sorry I'm late," I began and then, stopped when I realised that no one in that seminar was normally in my seminar with Miss Maggie Dale.

In place of the usual faces, there was Ben, a very tall guy with floppy blond hair that fell partly over his eyes. At six foot four, lean and well-built with attractive features, he looked like a male model and from his self-assured air, you could see that he knew it! What was HE doing in my seminar?

Come to think of it, what were any of them doing in my seminar, this sea of strange faces, none of whom belonged in my morning seminar with Maggie. Where were all the people who were normally in my seminar? Why had they all been replaced by these strangers? What was going on?

Then, it dawned on me. What if they're not all in the wrong seminar? What if I am? What if it's me who's in the wrong place?

My eyes fell on two faces that were familiar, the faces of Lara and Cheryl and so I ended my initially bold apology, *"Sorry I'm late..." with a lame, "......or am I.... in the wrong seminar?"*

"Dani, you're in the wrong seminar!" laughed Cheryl as Lara smiled at me sympathetically.

Embarrassment flooded over me. The first time I tried to be a new assertive me, I had made a fool of myself, bursting into the wrong seminar, someone else's seminar where I had no right to be!

"Oh! I'm sorry!" I squeaked. *"Sorry about that!"* and with that, I turned on my heel and scurried out of the room to peals of laughter that followed me out of the door!

Later that afternoon, I was informed by Cheryl and Lara that by bursting into the wrong seminar and providing light relief,

I had diffused tension and calmed a heated argument that had been brewing between Lara and Ben.

Apparently, they had been discussing Don Juan and Ben had been all in favour of Don Juan's Lothario-like, womanising ways while Lara, the Conservative Christian had been scathing in her criticism.

A hostile argument had been brewing between the two when I burst in through the door like a clueless clown and broke the tension by making everyone laugh!

"You were so funny, Danita. You burst into the lesson, apologising profusely for being late to a seminar you weren't supposed to be in, and once you realised your mistake you scurried out so fast, it was as if you thought that no one would notice if you sped out fast enough!"

That was Lara.

"You broke the tension between Ben and Lara and made us all laugh. You saved the day!" Cheryl added.

While I was happy that I had diffused the tension between Ben and Lara, turning up half an hour early and apologising for being late, playing the clown had knocked my confidence and it would be quite some time before I would try being "assertive" again!

Chapter Nineteen- Pop Mobility

After a couple of terms of being at university, I became well-settled into a routine.

Thursday at noon at the Sports Centre, I went to Pop Mobility classes. It was basically a group of mainly female students following an exercise routine to the sound of pop music.

On two podiums stood the instructors, a couple of mature students in their twenties, Paul and Wendy who modelled the moves that we followed for the hour-long session.

It was at pop mobility classes that I met Karishma and Simone. These were two, tall, statuesque girls who I met in the second week of the first term when I had started Pop Mobility.

Karishma and Simone looked like a pair of supermodels to me. Karishma had long, silky black hair that she tied up in a high pony tail that swung from side to side as she worked out, golden brown skin and a lean frame and Simone had long brown hair that she also tied up in a high pony tail but the most attractive thing about her were her wide, expressive brown eyes and her warm, friendly smile.

"Hi. I'm Dani. I'm a first-year student doing English and American Literature. Are you first years?" I asked at our first meeting.

"No, we're second-year students, living off campus. I'm Simone."

"And, I'm Karishma."

And that's how it started, our friendship at Pop Mobility Class.

I was in awe of the two slightly older girls because they had an air of sophistication that I didn't have. They were like proper, self-assured women whereas I got treated like a little school girl and I still felt like one.

I was the kind of girl that boys called "cute," whereas Karishma and Simone would be called stunning or beautiful.

"Oi! You lot! Dani's so cute, she could be the hall mascot!" Craig had exclaimed one day while watching football on TV in Rob's room.

He'd never say that about Karishma and Simone.

When these two willowy girls turned up at my halls of residence one day, these two normally cocky boys were suddenly on their best behaviour. I saw how they followed my two beautiful friends with their eyes. They suddenly looked all sweet and shy. I saw the effect these girls had on men. They only had to enter a room and all eyes would be on them.

Although I was initially intimidated, over the weeks, a friendship developed between me and them. At one point, they even took me back to their place and made me a home-cooked meal as if I were their little sister when they realised that I had been eating beans on toast and baked potatoes for weeks on end.

"Paul's looking rather dishy this morning," remarked Simone one morning as she eyed the very fit, fitness instructor in all his sporty finery doing his stretches on the podium.

Paul, we had discovered, was a mature student of twenty-six who was funding his Sports Science postgraduate degree by doing fitness instruction three days a week.

So, for three days a week, he stood there before us on his podium, flexing his pecs, looking resplendent in his bright, shiny Spandex cycling shorts.

Then, one day, it happened, something amazing, something that was the dream of every hormonal female teen.

Paul stepped off his pedestal, his podium and he headed for his teenage fans who followed his every move every week and guess who he came and stood next to?

Guess!

ME! Little me!

Did he stand next to the sultry and stunning Karishma with her long, lean physique and swinging ponytail? No.

Did he stand next to the imposing and gorgeous Simone with her warm smile and her magnetic eyes? No.

Who did he come and stand next to, this 1990's Adonis in Spandex cycling shorts? He stood next to ME, a teenager who still pulled her long socks up over her knees like a schoolgirl and who had only just learned to use a cash machine!

For the next exercise, we were told over the tannoy that we had to hold hands with the person next to us and skip around in a circle and guess who was standing next to me? Adonis himself in cycling shorts!

Reader, I wish I could tell you I held hands with the handsome Paul, skipped around with him in a circle, looked deeply into his eyes, fell in love and married him! But reader, I didn't marry him.

Reader, I ran! I ran away from the handsome man! I ran!

Remember, I was just a little girl from an all-girls school who only knew how to scream at posters of gorgeous men and get hysterical. I had never actually had the courage to hold hands with one!

I thought, "Oh my God! He's so nice. I can't hold his hand! I can't hold his hand and skip around with him in a circle. I'll faint!"

My heart was thumping wildly. Actually, it was doing somersaults. Little, timid me, I couldn't possibly hold the hand of a gorgeous man. I ran!

Later, I received a hearty telling off from Karishma who scolded both Simone and me, because despite her stunning beauty, it turned out that Simone was a nervous Nelly like me and had been struggling for months to say "hello" to a man she fancied, a man called Luigi!

"You two are chicken sh.t!" Karishma had rebuked us, scornfully.

"You're hopeless with men!"

So, I ran away from the gorgeous Paul because I was shy. I couldn't say "hello" to Daniel because I was scared so I wrote poems about his sneezes instead behind his back!

How was I ever going to get on in life if I couldn't even hold the hand of a man I liked?

While the Beatles sang robustly and bravely, "I wanna hold your hand," back in the sixties when my parents' generation was young, I couldn't even hold the hand of a nice man in Pop Mobility. I ran!

How on earth was I ever going to find a man?

Chapter Twenty- Misogyny

Simone wasn't just beautiful on the inside. She was beautiful on the inside as well. Her sweet, gentle nature was the best thing about her but I was about to find out that there was another side to the gentle Simone when provoked.

This gentle girl, I found, could be fiery when she witnessed abuse, when she felt that someone was being wronged.

I witnessed this side to her personality one evening when walking through the "Airport Lounge" with her up at the students' union.

The Airport Lounge wasn't really an airport lounge. It was part of the students' union. It was called the Airport Lounge because it looked like one!

Hundreds of students were relaxing with friends after a long week of lectures and seminars, getting bevvies in and there was an air of excitement in the air because it was the weekend of the cup finals.

You could hear chants of *"England and Engerland!"* as we walked through the hordes of students that thronged around the Flat screen TV in the lounge.

As Simone and I were passing through a quieter part of the union, I spotted a couple of Asian men who looked unfamiliar. I had never seen them before on our campus. They seemed out of place in our students' union somehow.

They had a menacing air about them and as I walked past, one of them swore at me in a menacing tone. Being a speaker of an Indian language at home, I knew he was insulting me but even though Simone had no knowledge of

Indian languages, she could tell from his tone that I was being abused.

This was when I saw a different side to my sweet, gentle, Anglo-Irish friend that I had never seen before. Quick as a flash, she strode over to these two bullies, her dark eyes, flashing fire as she demanded angrily,

"Do you speak to your mother with that mouth? Is this how you treat women? What gives you the right to abuse my friend?"

The two Asian men's jaws dropped open. They had not expected this.

Simone's fury had an unexpected effect. The two men apologised to her.

"No, don't apologise to me. Apologise to my friend!" was her angry reply as she pointed to me.

Then, she strode over to me and said,

"They can't stand to see an Asian girl, dressed up, going out with her Western friends of an evening. They want to monitor and control all Asian women as if they're their personal property and keep them tied to the kitchen sink!"

I was astonished that Simone knew so much about these types of Asian men. I had no idea that Asian men like this existed. I had no idea why they had felt the need to insult me while I had been minding my own business and not giving them a second thought.

I had never grown up in an Asian community so I had no idea that attitudes like this existed. Divorce had made my single-parent mother somewhat of a pariah among her own people back in the early eighties and we mixed with only two or three Asian families because of the stigma. As a result, I had never lived in an Asian area. I had no idea that there was a class of Asian men with this kind of pre-historic misogynistic mentality!

"Karishma had trouble with some of the Asian men too when she joined Asian Society," Simone confided in me. "They upset her so much, calling her Karishma the stripper when she wore a mini skirt to a meeting that she ran out in tears and never went back!"

Well, I wasn't wearing a miniskirt. I never wore mini-skirts. I never wore anything sleeveless or low cut so why were they picking on me? Was it my Levi 501 cut-offs with a long-sleeved T-shirt and trainers that had set them off? Why were these complete strangers obsessing about me and picking on me just because of my ethnicity?

I don't drink. I don't smoke. I don't have boyfriends. I can't even hold the hand of a cute guy even when I have the chance to. I just write poems about them when they sneeze in lectures. What right did these Asian misogynists have to make assumptions about me just because I was wearing Western clothes, someone Western born?

I would come to learn in the years to come that a certain class of Asian male viewed Asian women as property to be monitored and controlled even if those women are independent strangers who have never taken a penny from them and they have no right to be in their lives.

In the years to come, I would learn that while racism from a minority of far-right extremists was a threat to me, there were extremists from my own ethnicity that could be a threat to me as well.

In addition to the threat of racism, as a woman of colour, I would one day, have to battle the threat of misogyny. Simone wouldn't always be there to do it for me.

Chapter Twenty One- Birthday

Before I knew it, eight months had passed since we all met for the first time in the communal dining room and it was time for my nineteenth birthday. I was going into the final year of my teens!

I decided to go home to see my mother on my birthday weekend. I wanted to talk to her about Daniel. Every time I came within the vicinity of the boy with the Byronic hair and piercing eyes, he would look over and at me and sit near me and my friends in lectures and every time, I had to look away because of the promise I had made to my mother that there would be no issues with boys.

After I'd had the birthday meal she'd cooked for me, the conversation went something like this,

"Mum, I think I like him. I want to go out with him."

"Nita, you can't go out with him. We agreed on this before I let you go away. We made a deal. No boyfriends. You know these white boys, they won't marry a brown girl. They'll just have fun but when it comes to marriage, they'll marry in their own culture and then, our people won't have you. They will say, "This is a bad girl. She had a boyfriend," and you will end up alone. Do you want to end up alone Danita? Do you want to end up alone?"

"No!"

"Then, be a good girl. Focus on your studies and when you have graduated, we will think about finding you a nice boy in the faith."

It all seemed so hopeless, my mother re-iterating the "no boyfriend" rule. Then, there was Mrs Harding's complaint about my generation, the Liquorice All Sorts generation,

"black going with white, white going with brown, brown going with black!"

On top of that, in lectures when we studied The Last of The Mohicans, they called love between people of different colours miscegenation as if loving someone of a different skin colour was a sickness, a disease, an unwanted condition.

It was all too much for a sensitive, timid teenager.

When I was travelling back to campus on the coach, I had tears in my eyes. Life felt grim. I wasn't sure I even wanted to live any more in a world where people were so narrow-minded but my world changed in an instant, the moment I stepped back into my halls of residence.

My first reaction was one of astonishment.

"What's happened to my door?"

I was greeted by a bright array of colours. Around my door were strung balloons of bright primary colours, red, yellow and blue.

And across my door was a massive banner on which was written "HAPPY BIRTHDAY DANITA!"

When I tried to open the door, it jammed and I looked down to see why. There was a massive wodge of envelopes stuffed under the door which turned out to be full of birthday cards!

In an instant, life switched from being hopeless, miserable and grim to being full of joy and love and hope and reasons to live. It was incredible how my perspective changed in an instant just because of the environment I was in!

Life felt worth living again, full of colour and love and fun the moment I stepped back onto campus and re-entered the bubble of student life that sheltered me from the grim realities of the real world outside.

How long though before the bubble burst and I was back in the real world having to grapple with all kinds of issues, toiling under the burden of social expectations, living a life of duty like my mother, coping, existing, enduring, surviving, striving to live up to everyone's expectations of me?

Chapter Twenty Two- Duty Versus Desire.

"Happy birthday Danikins!" Emma's blue-grey eyes twinkled merrily as she handed me my present.

Impatiently, I tugged at the Sellotape that she'd used to wrap the notebook and pen ensconced within pink wrapping paper with a pretty floral design.

"Thanks, Em. That's just what I needed for my lecture notes. Thank you. You shouldn't have. A card would have been enough!"

"You're welcome Danikins."

Emma flashed me one of her warm smiles but the smile was soon replaced by a look of genuine concern.

"Dani, you look so sad. Why? What's wrong?"

"Nothing."

I tried to shrug it off. I shook my head and smiled back at her but she wasn't convinced.

"It's not nothing. I can tell from the look in your eyes. You're so transparent Danita. I can read you like a book. What's wrong? You can tell me. You can tell Aunty Emma."

I sighed a long-drawn-out sigh. She knew me too well. I couldn't lie to Emma.

"It's my mother. She expects me to be perfect all the time. I'm not allowed to date, to fall in love or have a boyfriend even though everyone around me is doing it. Everyone around me is free to do what they want but I have to live up to her expectations, God's expectations, society's expectations and to do my duty. Life is never fun for me. It's never about how I feel. I have to always put God and duty first, live for duty and put duty above desire and I'm only nineteen. Sometimes, it gets hard. It gets really hard."

Emma's brows furrowed into a frown.

"So, if you can't fall in love, if you can't date, if you can't have a boyfriend, how do you find someone?"

"My mum had an arranged marriage."

"What's that?"

"It's when your parents find you someone."

"So, did it work for your mum?"

"Nope."

"So, why would it work for you?"

"She says that I don't have to have an arranged marriage like her. She says I can choose but it has to be someone in the faith. I have to put God first."

"Would you marry someone you didn't love?"

"No way!"

"Did your mum love your dad?"

"No, she had an arranged marriage to someone she didn't even know. Apparently, lots of men liked her when she was young but she was shy and unconfident so when she was 27, they told her she had to get married because she had sisters who were younger and they couldn't get married until she did. The eldest has to go first so she did her "duty" and married someone she didn't love so that her younger sisters could get married."

Emma sighed and shook her head.

"Your poor mum."

"I know. You know my mum's friend got engaged at nineteen and she didn't know the facts of life at nineteen! She thought she was pregnant because her fiancé breathed on her. She said to my mum, *"I think I'm pregnant. He got too close to me. He breathed on me. It's going to be a scandal!"* She thought you could get pregnant from someone breathing on your face!

It wasn't just Indian women of my mum's generation either. Simone said her aunty went around telling everyone she was pregnant after she got married even though she and her husband hadn't done anything yet! Apparently, her husband was really embarrassed when she went around telling everyone she was pregnant because he knew she couldn't be!"

"Didn't they have sex education at school back in those days?"

"I'm guessing NOT! I was eleven when I found out before they gave us the talk at school."

"How?"

"Two other kids told me in the school playground."

"My cousin Amelia told me," said Emma. "She was two years older. So, how did Simone's aunt finally find out?"

"I think her husband had to tell her!"

"Hilarious. Poor man."

"I know. I wonder what my mother's generation did on their wedding night. They weren't allowed to have boyfriends. They weren't allowed to date. They didn't know the facts of life so what did they do on their wedding night, I wonder."

"God knows," replied Emma.

"What would a love-starved woman of twenty seven who doesn't know the facts of life do on her wedding night? All her life, she's been forbidden from having a man and when she finally gets one, she doesn't know what to do with him so what would she do? What would she do?

You know Em, I have this image in my mind of a twenty-seven-year-old Indian bride in all her bridal finery saying, "At last! At last! I have a man! Then, she gets all excited and leaps into the air like a Ninja and lands on the bed, saying, "HAIYAAH!"

Unsure what to do with herself, she launches herself at the poor, terrified groom, grabs hold of his face between her two hands, squeezes it, and rubs her nose with his furiously, thinking that THIS is how you make a baby!

After that, she lies back contentedly and says, "Oh! I feel pregnant! I feel pregnant! I just know we just made a baby! I'm going to have to call my mother in the morning to let her know that she's going to be a grandma." Then, just as she's about to fall asleep contentedly, the groom whispers something in her ear and she sits up bolt upright and says angrily,

"WHAT? WHAAAT? WHAT do you mean that's not how you make a baby?"

The poor bridegroom looks at her in abject terror, realising he's going to have to explain the facts of life to her while her eyes narrow in suspicion as she asks,

"Are you saying that my brother is a liar?"

The man replies nervously, *"N...no."*

So, she responds, *"Well then! Goodnight!"* And then, she promptly falls asleep and begins to snore!"

Emma laughed.

"You're funny Danikins."

"I'm not kidding Em. That's how I imagine my mother's generation on their wedding night- totally clueless. I'm surprised my parents were able to have me! You should see the old Indian movies from their time. When the man and woman fall in love, they dance around a tree on a mountain-top! Can you blame me for being clueless about the opposite sex? I'm descended from THESE people!"

"Maybe, the mountain is symbolic."

"What do you mean Em?"

"I mean that maybe they're saying that they feel like they're on top of the world when they find the one, when they fall in love like the song, Top of the World, the Carpenters Song."

"Maybe. You know Em. You might be right. Maybe the mountain is symbolic! Spoken like a true student of English lit!"

"Well, whatever you do Danikins, make sure when you get married, it's to someone you love. I couldn't bear the thought of you marrying someone you don't love just to please everyone."

"Don't worry Em. I'd rather be alone than be with the wrong man. My mum says that I don't have to have an arranged marriage. She says I can choose but he has to be of the faith because I have to put God first."

"Oh well, that narrows it down! I hope you find someone like my Bryan."

"I hope so too. Everything comes so easy to you Em. You're not a minority within a minority trying to find someone right for you from a narrow pool. You and Bryan are so well-matched like your matching suitcases, Flopsy and Mopsy. You're such a cute couple. You're so lucky to have found your soul-mate so young just like your parents. I love hearing your stories about your parents, about how they met so young at school and knew that they'd found the one. They're so lucky and so are you. I hope I get lucky like you someday."

"You will Danikins. You will. You're such a lovely girl. You're bound to have a glorious life!"

Emma's words were so kind and so hopeful but I'm not sure that I will ever be lucky and find true love, not with my luck.

Emma is ever optimistic because her life has taught her that life can be fun, that life can be wonderful. My life has taught me something different from the start.

I haven't come from a happy home like Emma where she took it for granted that her parents loved each other having been teenage sweethearts and each other's first love. My parents didn't even like each other. I wasn't born out of love like she was. I don't come from a happy home with parents who love each other with a loving younger brother and an adoring dog that gets excited every time I get home and greets me with a wagging tail and sticks his nose through the letter box to greet me when he knows I've come home.

I come from a broken home with no siblings, no pets, the child of an arranged marriage that ended in divorce, a marriage that was loveless.

Why would I expect to be lucky like Emma? Why would I expect to find true love?

Chapter Twenty Three- Emma

At a desk in a student bedroom sits a girl by lamplight, her russet curls tumbling around her shoulders and as she sits at her desk, she is writing a letter and here is what it says:

Dear Mum

I hope you, Dad, Alex and Ben are well. I'm looking forward to seeing you all in July once exams are done.

I can't believe the first year is nearly over. Time has flown so fast. I guess I must be having fun although it wasn't much fun yesterday. I had a terrible day in class.

We're coming to the end of teaching practice, thank God! The kids were all behaving so oddly. They all kept laughing at me as I stood in front of the classroom beside the board and I couldn't understand why!

I was using my stern, teacher-like, authoritarian tone which usually works but not yesterday. I couldn't get them to take me seriously at all!

Then, one of them told me why.

"Miss, you've got chalk on the end of your nose!"

I must have looked so silly Mum, standing there, trying to be taken seriously by a class of ten-year-olds with chalk on the end of my nose! No wonder the kids kept laughing at me! Has that ever happened to you?

I'd been doing so well before that. I had come so far from the first few weeks of teaching practice when I was so nervous, I kept making mistakes. You know Mum how I make mistakes when I'm nervous. Well, I put my foot in it, calling a little girl Tuna! Her name's Tina and I called a little boy Florence! His name's Laurence! They both got teased because of it and Tina said to me,

"I was always Tina before YOU came here Miss!"

I felt terrible. You know how I get my words muddled when I'm nervous!

Anyway, after yesterday's fiasco, I'm always going to keep a compact mirror with me in my handbag to make sure I don't have chalk on the end of my nose!

Oh, and Mum, do you remember I told you about my Indian friend, Danita? Well, guess what? Her mum had an arranged marriage to a complete stranger, a man she didn't love! Can you believe that? Her dad never loved her mum. Imagine growing up in a home where your parents don't love each other and barely tolerate each other. I've always taken my life for granted. I never will again, now that I know how sad some other people's lives are.

Some months ago, when we were picking our favourite Carpenters Song, I picked Top of the World and at the age of eighteen, Danita picked Goodbye to Love. I mean, how sad is that? Maybe, it's the difference in our upbringing. I'm ever the optimist while she just expects bad things to happen in her life.

Plus, she's always making gaffes where men are concerned. She's so naïve, she takes everything at face value. She's like a child. She reminds me of that song by Cat Stevens, you know the one? Wild World! She's like the girl in the song. That should be her signature tune! She's totally naïve, totally green. How is she going to survive in the world being so naïve and so green? I worry about her sometimes! I hope she doesn't have an arranged marriage like her mother.

I hope she finds someone nice like Bryan or dad and lives happily ever after.

I'm missing you Mum. Give my love to Dad, Alex and Ben. I can't wait to see you all again especially Ben! He's always the first to greet me when I get home sticking his nose through the letter box, barking madly and wagging his tail!

See you all soon, next month after my exams!

Lots of love

From

Emma

Chapter Twenty Four- Time Flies!

They say, "Time flies when you're having fun!" Well, I must have been having great fun in my first year because before I knew it, it was nearly over!

Gone was the trepidation of those first few weeks, those early days when we all tiptoed around each other in the communal areas of our hall of residence, trying to make a good impression.

Over the months, familiarity set in and we bonded as a group. Formalities were set aside and the fluffy slippers came out!

It had been months since that first jelly fight when the stern and slightly terrifying hall warden, Parminder had swooped on our corridor and taken our group to task over the jelly on the walls!

Now, in the summer, some of us were turning up to lectures after water fights, dripping wet! There was a heady feeling of being young and on the threshold of life, a new generation just about to emerge, take off and test its wings.

The first-year exams didn't count towards our final grade but we still had to get a passing grade to move on up to the second year.

So, revision had to be done. I tried not to leave everything until the last minute as I had done in the first term of my first year when I had pulled an all-nighter, trying to read all of Shakespeare's sonnets in one night. I had sonnets coming out of my ears! It was not an experience I ever wanted to repeat again!

In the last year of my teens, I felt like a child-woman, veering more on the side of being a girl rather than a woman! My diet consisted of beans on toast, beans on baked potatoes, Ocean burgers and chips bought at the students' union and a smattering of fruit and veg as my concerned mother was always sending me letters, nagging me to eat healthily and not to have junk food like burgers and chips every day!

Then, there was the soup machine in the students' union and although the soup it dispensed was thin and watery, it was hot and it had little bits of carrot and green veg floating around in it which made me feel virtuous because carrot bits could be considered healthy-ish or so I thought at the time!

We had four papers to sit in the first year, Epic Literature covering Ancient Greek literature, The Iliad, the Odyssey, the Aeneid and then, there was Medieval literature going back to Chaucer and Gawain and the Green Knight whose author was unknown. Deciphering ancient English was like deciphering another language altogether. It was not easy!

The other papers were International Modern Literary Studies or IMLS and Poetry.

I was a veteran at doing exams by the age of eighteen and I always had exams around the time of my birthday, having been a June baby! I felt my parents should have planned my conception better and had me in August during the time of my summer holidays instead of dragging me into the world in the month of June so that I could have exams around the time of every important birthday!

As an exam veteran, when I saw the neat rows of desks in the main hall with the name labels, it was like being back at high school.

We all left our bags at the front as hawk-eyed invigilators monitored our every move.

Having breakfasted on toast and watery soup, I felt as ready as I ever would be to take my first-year exams.

In the IMLS exam, there was a character called Boris Yeltsin.

I wrote in the exam about Boris Yeltsin's "Transworld identity" which basically means that he is a real person from the real world who is presented as part of someone's fictional story. I did this because I felt sure I'd heard the name Boris Yeltsin mentioned somewhere as someone from the real world but then, I panicked because I couldn't be sure!

So, after I left the exam room when the exam had ended, I ran over to Rob and Craig in the Airport Lounge, crying,

"Craig! Rob! Boris Yeltsin! Is he alive? Is he alive? Is he a real person? I need him to be a real person to get my marks in my exam! Is he real? Is he real?"

Craig knows a lot about politics because he's doing a degree in English and Politics so I made a beeline for him!

To my relief, Craig nodded and said,

"Yep. He sure is! He's a politician in Russia."

I breathed a sigh of relief.

"Thanks, Craig. I knew you'd know."

Craig's lips curved into a smile.

"No worries Dani mate. If you've got any questions, you can ask me. Ask Uncle Craig any time! I'm a walking, talking encyclopaedia, me!"

And Craig was right. He WAS like a walking, talking encyclopaedia! A brilliant brain lay behind those sharp, eagle eyes that never missed a detail for Craig was a genius in disguise.

Later that evening, when we all went up to the students' union together as we did every Friday night, we celebrated the end of exams because the first year was over and we were all going home at the weekend for the summer.

Chapter Twenty Five- Typos

An office in a busy metropolis. A middle-aged man is sitting opposite a young man at a desk in a small office.

"Rob, son, I'm going to have to let you go."

"But Uncle Jack, I need this job. I need the money and I need the experience on my CV."

The middle-aged man sighs deeply and shakes his head.

"Son, I can help you out with money if that's what you need. I know it's been tough for you since... since your father... but I can't keep you on..."

"But Uncle Jack..."

The middle-aged man shakes his head with firm determination.

" Look son, I've got a firm to run and your mind is clearly not on the job. I've given you chance after chance but here we are again. You've got to focus kid. Your mind's never on the job. This is a law firm, not a charity. We can't have these kinds of errors. You've done this too many times. You need to get your head out of the clouds, son.

I mean look at these mistakes. You've typed here International Bonking Conference!"

"I meant International Banking Conference, Uncle Jack."

Rob looked at Uncle Jack, his summer employer with a stricken expression on his childlike face. The stricken look was followed by a deep sigh.

"Rob, that was just one of many mistakes, lad. This has just kept on happening.

There was the sign that you typed up that said, "No smoking in pubic areas."

"I meant "No smoking in public areas Uncle Jack."

Uncle Jack sighed and shook his head.

I ignored the application letter in which you wrote, *"I enjoy working in busty environments,"*

"I meant busy environments."

"So, why didn't you say that then son? How many times have I reminded you to proofread what you write, lad?"

Rob sighed again, looking contrite. *"Sorry, Uncle Jack."*

"You always are son. What about this one when you wrote that working at her employers damaged our client's elf-esteem?"

"I meant self-esteem."

"So, write that then, son. Then, there was the time when you wrote that someone had been throwing thongs in the lobby!"

"Things...I meant things!"

And the worst one, the absolute worst one for which I have to let you go Robbie my lad is the letter in which you described our client Steve Jones as the rapist! We nearly got sued after that one! What on earth were you thinking son?"

Rob winced and bit his lip before responding,

"I meant, Steve Jones, therapist Uncle Jack but I must have accidentally touched the space button in the middle of the word."

"Well, that's not good enough son. You could have landed us in a lot of trouble if Steve hadn't accepted my apology and agreed to let it go!"

Uncle Jack sighed, his brow furrowed...

"You're a good kid, Robbie, lad. I wanted to give you this chance because I know what you and your mum have been through but I can see you're really not up to it right now, not with everything you've been through. You're my sister's kid and I want the best for you. You know that but right now, what's best for you is therapy. You need to work through your issues, son. Your mind's just not on the job. You need to sort yourself out. I'll give you a month's pay to help you and your mum out but I have to let you go son. You have to understand."

Rob sighed, his face a picture of misery. Uncle Jack softened. He stood up. He walked round to his nephew's side of the desk and put a reassuring arm on his shoulder.

"It's not the end of the world lad. There will be other jobs but right now, you need to sort yourself out. You've been through a major trauma. If you need money, I'll be here to support you and your mother. After all, your mum's my little sister. I won't see you or her go short. I'm always here when you need me. You know that son. You know you can depend on your Uncle Jack."

Uncle Jack looked into Robin's ocean-blue eyes which looked startlingly like his own.

"All right son?"

Rob nodded.

"All right Uncle Jack."

"You work on sorting yourself out and next summer, once you've got your head sorted, we'll try again. It's only been a short time since you know.... You need time to get your head round what's happened, get some support and we'll try again next summer. All right son?"

The older man hugged the younger one and then, ushered him gently out of the office.

Later that evening, one Robin Martin called his friend, Craig Johnson on the phone.

"Hello?"

"Hi Craig? It's Rob."

"Oh, Rob. Hey mate. What gives?"

"I got the sack. My Uncle Jack let me go. He said my head's not in the right place. I made too many typos, embarrassing ones so he's had to let me go."

"Well, it's only been a while since your dad..."

"I know."

"You need to take it easy mate."

Rob sighed deeply on the phone.

"I wanted to earn some money over the summer."

"Can you manage on what you've got?"

"Well, Uncle Jack said he'd help me and Mum out if we're really struggling."

"Why don't you come over from Leeds to Liverpool? Come and stay with me and me Nan. She'd love to meet you."

"I'd love to only I promised I'd help out in a local soup kitchen for the homeless as a volunteer."

"That's just like you Rob to be a bleeding-heart volunteer for the poor. You're a working-class hero our Rob. That's what you are."

On the other side of the line, Rob smiled, a pained expression on his face and as he put the phone down some minutes later, there were tears, glistening, in his ocean-blue eyes.

Chapter Twenty Six- Summer Job

It was my mother's idea for me to help out over the summer at a local play-scheme.

"Danita, you need some work experience to put on your CV, so why don't you go and work at Mrs Ahmed's play-scheme? She's not asking for experience. She just wants some teenagers to help out with the kids. Why don't you go?"

So, I went. I needed work experience. Volunteering was a good way to get it. I interviewed for the position and once my police check came through, I got the job.

Suddenly, I found myself surrounded by other teenage helpers and lots of lively little kids.

I had to help them with reading, writing, basic arithmetic, times tables. I had to play board games with them, watch over them while they were playing in the garden and basically, be like a big sister to them and keep them safe.

The play-scheme was run by a local Asian woman who had hired lots of Asian students like me who were trying to get some work experience on their holiday. I volunteered for the play-scheme for four weeks and it was an eye-opening experience. Some of the girls I worked with seemed to think they had a right to tell other people how to dress, what to believe, and how to live.

"Why don't you wear Asian clothes like the salwar kameez? Why don't you take pride in your own culture?" was one question thrown at me.

"Aren't you proud of your Asian heritage?" was another.

I was astonished at their line of questioning. I had been born in Britain and raised here so why would they give me a hard time for wearing Western clothes like a long-sleeved T-shirt and jeans as opposed to salwar kameez?

A couple of them gave me such a hard time over wearing Western clothes so imagine my surprise when I found out that the ones who had given me a hard time had boyfriends coming over when their parents were away to smoke dope with them! They were traditional on the outside and preaching to others while there was something else going on inside!

By contrast, I was dressing in Western clothes but I didn't have a boyfriend and I didn't touch intoxicants! How ironic that they looked traditional but weren't and I looked Western but towed the line. I learned that appearances could be deceptive from being around some of these girls.

Their need to control others didn't stop at criticising people for their clothing either. I nearly died of embarrassment when they picked on a woman working at the play-scheme for her religion!

One of the teenage helpers, Salma verbally accosted a Hindu woman who was working with us in front of the children!

This was the one who strutted round the place in stiletto heels and salwar kameez as if she owned the place and used the f... word in front of the children! I think she was Mrs Ahmed's niece and felt entitled as she was related to the boss!

"Why are you a Hindu?" she said tactlessly to my colleague. "Why aren't you a Muslim? Can't you see it makes sense?"

I felt embarrassed being a Muslim that day. How could this bully represent me? It says in the Quran,

"To you your religion and to me, my religion."

And

"There is no compulsion in religion."

In other words, you can't force others to believe as you believe. Everyone needs to make their own choices in life because life is a test and you can't expect someone else to sit your test for you!

A couple of the girls at the play-scheme were different to my friends at university. They were nosy. They lacked tact and they could be rude.

The woman they had verbally harassed had a nephew and a niece at the play-scheme and they had verbally abused her in front of them. Embarrassment didn't even begin to cover how I felt when they did that in front of the children.

Rupa was an adorable little eight-year-old girl with bright, shining, dark eyes, a little heart-shaped, angelic face and a cute little button nose and her brother, Avi was equally adorable and just four years of age.

On one occasion when he fell and scraped his knee, he was about to cry but bit his lip and held back his tears when he saw how distraught I was when I thought he was hurt. He was a little man worrying about other people's feelings even when hurt himself at just four years of age!

If we believed in past lives in my religion, I would have thought that we had been family in a past life because the bond between me, Rupa and Avi was instant.

Walking in the park with the playgroup holding Rupa's hand and with little Avi on my back, it hit me really hard,

"THIS must be what it feels like to have a family!"

I felt so serene, holding this little girl's hand and giving her baby brother a piggy back as if they were my siblings. For an instant, this lonely only child got to be a big sister. I had never felt so bonded to anyone like this other than my own mother.

Rupa clearly felt it too because when were back in the building after our jolly jaunt in the park, she leaned her little head against my arm and looked up with those bright, shining, innocent eyes and sighed before saying wistfully,

"I wish you were my big sister."

Then, all of a sudden, her eyes lit up and she said,

"I'm going to ask my Mummy to adopt you! I think my Mummy wants to adopt a big girl!"

"I think your mummy would have something to say about that!" my mother objected after I told her about the charming little girl who felt as if she could be my own baby sister.

Her words touched my heart though because I had always hated being an only child and had longed for years for a baby brother or sister.

There were times when as a little girl myself, I had longed for a big sister, someone warm and loving who would scoop me up in a warm hug, someone who would take me out for days out when Mum was struggling with depression and money worries as a single parent, someone who would make a fuss of me and let me know that I was loved.

At the age of ten, I had a scrap book of Lady Diana, the kind girl who went around hugging everyone. Rupa had looked up at me the way I had looked up to her when I was a little girl. It was like history repeating itself, little girls looking up to big girls, longing for the love of a big sister.

Single parent mothers who have experienced domestic violence and the stigma of divorce can end up with depression—depression that makes them lose their tempers with their bewildered kids, depression that stops them from being able to show love to their children.

Imagine being a single parent's child who has no father and no siblings. That child only has a mother who is damaged by trauma. That one person they have can't show love because she's depressed even though she loves her child. That was me for years.

I would be in my early twenties before I realised just how much my mother loved me. That was after I had spent years in my teens trying to be perfect and had ended up with anorexia and bulimia, trying to be worthy of being loved!

Walking through that park, feeling serene with these two younger kids, I suddenly knew what it felt like to have a real family with siblings, to have that sibling bond I never had and would never have. These two little children felt like family to me. The bond between us was instant and real.

How I hated having to say "goodbye" to the two little children who had won my heart, knowing I would never see them again, two people who had given me a glimpse of how it felt to be part of a loving family. I had a feeling that no matter how much time passed, those children would have a permanent place in my heart.

Chapter Twenty Seven – The Spectrum

When the new term began, I found myself in a house living with other Muslim girls. This had not happened by chance. All of us had been forbidden by our parents from living in houses with boys. So, we had all had to opt for an all-female house.

My other friends who had no such religious restrictions were living in mixed houses where there were boys as well as girls. Emma, Chrissie and Lara had given me the option of living with them but I had to turn them down because of the "no-boy" rule laid down by my mother.

So, here I was, living in a house with strangers, people I barely knew, girls I had met at the Asian Society who had found themselves in the same predicament as me thanks to the "no boys" rule laid down by their parents as well.

In my second year of university, I lived off campus with Amina, Asma and Sophia. Asma was studying Medicine while Amina was studying Sociology and Sufia or Sophie as we called her, was studying English Literature with me.

The contrast between Amina, Asma and Sophie couldn't be greater. They were at the opposite ends of the Muslim spectrum!

Asma was small, serious-minded and studious. Never one to go out of an evening, she mainly stayed at home after dark just as I did when back at home with my mother in London. When she did venture out, she wore a scarf even at nineteen years of age.

Amina was similar to Asma but she was much more talkative than Asma when surrounded by people she knew while Sophie, my other housemate, was the total opposite to my two new shy and retiring house-mates. Sophie was an extrovert who was out every Saturday night. She was not averse to a little tipple now and again and unbeknown to her parents, she was dating. She had a boyfriend.

In between these two opposite extremes, there was me in the middle. "No drinking, no smoking, no boyfriends, no pork." I kept the promise I had made to my mother but while I was more restrained than Sophia, I was less strict than Asma and Amina in other ways.

I wore Western fashions, no headscarf, and I did attend the occasional bop or disco with my native friends. I was still close to native friends I had made on my course and in my hall of residence the year before.

"Dani, where were you last night?" Emma called out from the steps of the Arts Centre as she beckoned me over.

I was waiting to cross the road to get to her and I yelled back, "I was at home last night, listening to my Olivia Newton John tape!"

Emma's eyes widened as I said this and she froze. Meanwhile, Lara ducked and hid her face behind a book as if I had said something wrong!

"What? Why are you looking at me like that?" I asked as I climbed the steps up to where they were sitting.

Emma's look was one that combined apology with embarrassment as she responded,

"Danikins, Olivia Newton John is really 1981 if you know what I mean."

"Huh?" I had no idea we couldn't admit to liking Olivia Newton John more now that Indie pop had taken over and Grunge was the in-thing.

I still liked her. I remember when Grease came out when I was seven and we all used to do the Olivia Newton John and John Travolta dance routine in the playground, singing, "You're the one that I want! You are the one I want! Ooh! Ooh! Ooh!"

I remember singing, *"You better shape up cos I need a man!"* and my mum saying in her Indian accent, " No, you don't need a man. You are only seven!"

"I really liked her Em when she was in Grease with John Travolta, remember? When we were kids..."

"I know Dan but that was in 1978 and we're not seven any more. The world has moved on."

"Well, I still like her. I know that now, everyone likes the Stone Roses and the Cure and the Smiths but I still like her. I don't see why we have to discard people when they're not considered fashionable any-more! Isn't that a bit shallow?"

"Well, there's a boy in our house who loves John Travolta's dance moves. You should get together with him sometime," suggested Lara.

I must have looked puzzled because Emma went on to explain,

"There's this boy called Jeff. He's a bit of a quiet one but last Saturday, when he thought we were all out, we caught him doing something hilarious in the kitchen when he thought he was alone."

"What did he do?" I asked all agog.

"Lara and I had left something behind so we'd come back into the house and we caught him in the kitchen doing this sudden dramatic spin with a really serious look on his face and then, he stuck his arm up in the air really dramatically when he thought that no one was looking.

And THEN, he started strutting around the kitchen with this intense look on his face like John Travolta in Saturday Night Fever! It was HILARIOUS!

Lara and I nearly died, laughing!"

"You're so mean to be laughing at the poor boy. He thought he was alone. I mean, how many of us hasn't done something silly when we're all alone?"

"I know but he was really funny. Maybe you and he should get together and have a tete a tete about John Travolta and your beloved Olivia Newton John."

"Well, I wouldn't go that far," I said smiling. "I do wish I was still living with you guys though because it sounds as if I'm missing out on all the fun."

Emma sighed and said,

"I know Danikins. We miss you too. Let's all apply to get back onto campus in the third year, apply early for the same hall of residence so we can all live together again."

"Agreed!" I said affably as we rose from the steps and headed towards the Humanities Building for the first lecture of the day.

Chapter Twenty Eight- House-warming.

A couple of weeks into term, it came, the invitation. The boys were having a house-warming party and we were all invited, me Lara and Emma and a few others from the hall of residence that we had all lived in during the first year.

Rob and Craig were sharing a house this year with two other lads, John and Andy. John was on the same course as Rob, English with Media Studies and Andy was reading English and Politics with Craig.

Emma and I showed up at 7 sharp with snacks and Lara arrived fashionably late an hour later with a bottle of budget wine.

The house was a regular terraced house with three bedrooms upstairs and a living room downstairs which they had turned into another student bedroom, opting to use the large dining area as a common living room.

To the left of us, as we entered, was the living room which was being used as a bedroom by Craig and just opposite us were the stairs.

The dining area was being used as a living space with a small sofa, a TV opposite the sofa and a dining table near the patio doors that led to the back garden. The galley kitchen and the stairs faced the front door.

As we entered, there were some students in the dining area, singing along to a tune that was being played on an acoustic guitar by Craig.

At the top of the stairs was a mysterious figure surrounded by smoke. The smoke machine had gone wrong we were told and as the mist cleared, we realised that the mysterious figure was Rob.

"Hi folks!" he called out cheerfully from the top of the stairs as the mist cleared and he became visible.

"Rob! Long time, no see!" I called up the stairs, "How have you been?"

Rob bounded down the stairs until he was standing just two feet away from us.

"Getting used to being back again, getting used to the new house and having to drive up to campus. Can't just roll out of bed now you know, now that we're off campus."

"I know what you mean," I sympathised. "We're all going to try and get back onto campus next year for the final year."

"Sounds like a good idea," Rob agreed after which he asked,

"Anyone want a drink?"

"Cider for me," said Emma.

"I'll have anything without alcohol in it," I responded.

Rob laughed as I said this.

"Oh yes! I remember you were the only one sober during our Friday night piss ups last year!"

Rob handed us our drinks and we all made our way into the dining area with the snacks where the action was, where the charismatic Craig strummed his guitar and half a dozen students thronged around him, having a sing-song.

"After that, Rob started blasting music from the 1980s and the 1970s from the speakers, and Lara and Emma had a good old dance to Abba, especially 'Dancing Queen.' They sang 'Aha!' in unison to the song 'Voulez Vous' as they paraded up and down the room dramatically. This was followed by 'Lay All Your Love on Me!' After that, the boys danced to 'The Stone Roses' and 'The Cure."

Later, that evening, we all ended up in Craig's room on the ground floor, dancing in a circle. We were all having such a great time when all of a sudden, Craig and Clare, one of the girls who had been in our hall of residence in the first year, went and laid down on his bed.

I thought to myself, "Aww, bless, they're having a little lie down because they're tired out from the dancing! Bless their little hearts."

Happy and content, I sat on the floor listening to UB40's Don't Break My Heart, hugging my knees, singing along to the words,

"Don't break my heart

Just remember,

It's the only one I've got

The only one I've got!"

Oddly, I noticed that one by one, the other students were leaving. I couldn't understand why.

"Why are they leaving when we're all having such a nice time?" I thought to myself.

I carried on singing happily, hugging my knees.

All of a sudden, Lara grabbed me by the wrist and pulled me out of the room as I protested,

"But Lara! The song hasn't finished yet!"

Lara didn't answer. She disappeared into the bathroom after having pulled me out of the room. She didn't look very happy.

"What's wrong with Lara?" I thought to myself. "That's not like her. Is she having a nervous breakdown or something? Why would she just yank me rudely out of the room? That's not like her! What's going on with her?"

Puzzled by this strange behaviour from Lara, I headed back for Craig's room but when I tried to turn the knob on the door, I found that the door was locked!

"Huh? What's up with people today? Fine! I know when I'm not wanted!" I thought crossly as I trudged up the stairs feeling quite perplexed to one of the bedrooms upstairs where Emma was sitting with Chrissie.

As soon as I entered the room, Emma asked,

"Dani, did you see Craig and Clare?"

"Yes," I replied non-plussed. "They were having a little lie down on Craig's bed. I think they were having a rest because they were tired out from the dancing."

Emma gave me a look that was inscrutable before she said,

"Danita, they were not having a little lie down or a rest."

She gave me a disapproving look. Then, she sighed and shook her head.

"What? What do you mean they weren't having a rest? You mean ... NO! But they're not married. I mean, they're not even a couple. She's not his girlfriend, is she? She's just a friend so why would they...?"

"It's called a one-night-stand Danikins. They are just friends. They're not a couple. They're not in love. They're just drunk. That's all. I expect they'll emerge from that room looking all embarrassed in the morning. Did you really think they were having a lie-down? Really?"

Now, it was my turn to be embarrassed. Everyone had been leaving the room while I had been sitting there, not taking the hint, thinking they were having a "little lie down!"

"Everyone must think I'm so silly. Silly Danita sitting there singing along to UB40 when everyone's leaving the room because Craig and Clare want to "get it on."

I felt such a "divvy" as Craig would say.

When was I ever going to learn how other people's minds worked? I still felt like a little school girl trying to make sense of an ever increasingly adult world!

Chapter Twenty Nine- Culture Confusion

Living in a house with other girls of my faith, I began to have two sets of friends, my native friends from my hall of residence in my first year and my minority friends who I had begun living with in the second year.

Despite being of the same faith background, we were a disparate bunch. Sophie was chatty and extrovert while Amina and Asma were introverts who wore the headscarf and never went out after dark.

I was the one in the middle of the spectrum. Like Sophie, I wore Western clothes and went to bops on campus with my female native friends but like Amina and Asma, I avoided alcohol and I didn't have boyfriends. I was trying to balance being both Eastern and Western. I had a foot in both worlds.

My mum and I had made a deal before she let me go to a campus university.

"No drinking, no smoking, no boyfriends, no pork but if you want to go out with female friends for a bit of innocent fun which doesn't involve boys or alcohol, that's OK. I don't want you sitting alone in your room for the time that you're there," my mother had said to me before letting me go.

I could have some fun but there was a line I could not cross. If I crossed that line, I couldn't come back. I would lose my place and she would suffer judgement for having let me go.

So, for the sake of my single parent mother who had done the job of both the mother and the father and who had sacrificed so much, putting me first, I had to toe the line.

So, here I was in an all-girl student house with three other girls who had widely differing in interpretations of what it meant to be a Western Muslim, born and raised in a Western country.

"How many brothers and sisters do you have?" Sophie had asked me when we first met.

"None. I'm a lonely only, I'm afraid," was my reply.

Sophie's eyes widened in astonishment.

"You're an only child! That's unusual for an Asian family."

"I guess so but that's my life. I used to beg my mum for a baby brother or sister but I never got one. My parents were mismatched from the start. They had me to see if it would bring them closer together. It didn't, so she never had another child because she knew it wasn't going to work out between them and she didn't want to bring another child into the mess."

"I'm sorry," Sophie sympathised.

"What about you? Do you have brothers or sisters?" I enquired.

"Three older brothers."

"Wow! One sister after three brothers! You must be a right little princess!"

"Not really. Brothers can be annoying. They're always obsessed with what you're doing and sticking their nose in their sister's business and they love teasing me because I'm the youngest and the only girl and they have no respect for my privacy. The number of times I've caught them reading my diary, it's not funny! They read it and then make fun of me for things I've written. They don't take me seriously."

"But your parent must adore you, their only girl."

"Well, yes. My dad's softer with me than he is with the boys although he can be a bit much sometimes. He made me throw out a perfectly good pair of pyjamas I bought because they had little cartoon pigs on them! I mean I know we're not supposed to eat anything from a pig but he wouldn't even let me wear pyjamas with little cartoon pictures of pigs on! They weren't even real pigs!"

"And your mum?"

"Oh, Mum and I have a special bond. We're the only two girls in the house. We're outnumbered by the men. We have mother and daughter only shopping days sometimes when we want to get away from them."

"That sounds like fun," I said.

"What about you and your parents?"

"Parent," I corrected her. "I only have one. My parents are divorced. I only have a mum. My father ran off when she asked for child support. The solicitors sent her a letter saying that the bailiffs couldn't find him at his normal address when they went to find him. He disappeared after my mother asked for child support."

Sophie frowned and shook her head.

"I didn't know that people behaved like that."

"Well, they do when money is involved. Some people do anyway."

"I'm sorry. It must be hard being just two people in a family, just you and your mum."

I shrugged.

"I don't know any different. I'm used to it. It's been just the two of us for so long."

"That's hard. I'm sorry."

"Don't be. That's life", I answered. "No one said it would be easy."

"So, what do you do to wind down and relax?"

"Mmm... Chrissie and I love Ella Fitzgerald, watercolour painting and dance and I love comedy. I used to want to be a comedienne. I used to watch Mike Yarwood and Tracey Ullman a lot as a kid. I loved them. I loved the way they make people laugh.

Then, there were all these sitcoms back in the seventies when I was born like George and Mildred and Mind Your Language.

I used to dream of being a comedienne and make silly radio shows or recordings at home with my friends from school. I even got on the radio once for doing a five-minute comedy skit. I love making people laugh.

I think it comes from being the new girl at school because my mum moved me around so much from the UK to Asia and back to the UK again. I found myself being the new girl a few times. It was hard to make friends when everyone had their cliques and friendship groups already. The way to get into those groups was to be funny. Everyone loves a funny girl."

"I had a feeling about you, Danita," said Sophie, smiling. "I think we're going to be great friends. I like people who make me laugh."

"Then, we should get along really well Sophie. I think we're going to have a great year."

And that was the beginning of our friendship. I could see that like Emma, Sophie had had a happy upbringing so she took it for granted that happiness was her lot in life. My friends had never known tragedy. It was something far away and distant for them, something that had never touched their lives.

I was glad that my friends had never known tragedy like me but sadly, for one of them, that was about to change.

Chapter Thirty- Sophie's Mistake

One of the things I noticed about Sophie was her fearlessness. She had no fear of life because life had never failed her. She was an eternal optimist because she had never known tragedy so she didn't feel that it applied to her. She had the boundless enthusiasm and optimism of a puppy. She had no fear of leaping into situations that nervous Nellies, hard-bitten by life at a young age, shied away from, nervous Nellies like me!

"You can't afford to make mistakes Danita. You are a child of divorce. Already that is a stigma and you don't have a father to pick you up if you fall. You have to be careful," was my mother's advice to me.

"People can spend their whole life paying for just one mistake," was another one.

So, I grew up terrified of making a mistake while Sophie had no such fear. Life had been a breeze for her so she didn't see any pitfalls. She was a warm-hearted girl with big, puppy-like brown eyes and a generous heart but she was naïve because she expected the world to always be kind.

I first realised how naïve she was when she confided in me about Terry, a boy she had met on her course.

"Dani, he's so nice. He's tall, gorgeous and he says he likes me. He really likes me but there is a problem..."

"What? What's the problem?"

"He's got a girlfriend back home and he doesn't want to tell her about me."

My eyes were like saucers when she said this to me. My reaction was visceral.

"WHAAT? Are you seriously considering going out with a love rat? If he can cheat on her Sophie, what's to stop him from cheating on you? Are you kidding me? Why would you even consider going out with someone like him?"

The soppy smile on Sophie's face disappeared at this. She looked chastened. She bit her lower lip and the beginnings of a frown furrowed her forehead.

"You're right Dani. You're right. I'll say no."

"Thank God!" I thought. "Thank God, she's seen sense!"

But not for long because, after Terry, there was Kevin. She introduced me to him one day on campus.

"Danita, you've got to meet him!" she gushed. "I think he's the one, the love of my life. He's so sweet. He's just so... sensitive! You've got to meet Kevin!"

So, she introduced me to the "sweet, shy and sensitive" Kevin who had a glassy look in his eyes as if he was high on drugs and he greeted me with a smirk, saying,

"I like your friend Sophie. Let's have a threesome."

Sensitive, my foot! What planet was she on?

How many times could I warn this naïve girl with the bouncy personality and wide, puppy dog eyes about the dangers of letting the wrong man into your life, a danger that my mother had warned me about so many times.

It seems the delights of Kevin wore off soon after that but then, Kevin was replaced by Nick.

This one let her down as well. This one had been sleeping around and had given her a health concern! She ended up in a clinic for treatment and looked ashen and drawn after taking the morning after pill. She didn't look like herself for a few days after that. She looked terrible.

Sophie's happy life being doted on by three older brothers and her happily married parents had left her with a feeling of being invulnerable. She was trusting of everyone.

At the opposite end of the spectrum, I had no confidence at all in relationships with the opposite sex. Thanks to my mother's tragic life and her constant warnings of danger, I had been left wary and afraid, unable to trust any man in case he tore my life apart in case I spent my whole life paying for one mistake as my mother had.

Two opposite extremes, two opposite ends of the pole and we were both called Muslim!

Sophie confided in me like a sister, and cautious person that I was, I tried to give her good advice to keep her safe.

At the end of the first term of our second year when we went home for the Christmas break, she promised that she would never be so overly trusting of boys again. She would be careful the next time but sadly, for Sophie, there was never going to be a next time...

When we returned to our shared student house in January, Sophie was gone. She never returned. After a week of trying to reach her on the phone, she finally sent me a letter telling me that she wasn't coming back!

Asma, Amina and I were in shock. Apparently, Sophie had confided to a friend back home about what had happened with Nick. That friend had confided in her sister who had confided in their mother who had then rung Sophie's mother to tell her what had happened to her daughter and the whole family had been in uproar with Sophie's father turning on her mother, blaming her for spoiling her and indulging her, their only daughter.

Her once doting brothers had stopped talking to her and her parents once happy marriage was dissolving under the strain of it all as her mother had decided to stand by her only daughter and stand against her father.

Her parents, who had once been happily married, were now getting a divorce! Sophia, whose world was once so solid and unshakeable was now becoming a child of divorce like me!

I wrote back to her, trying to comfort her but what could I say that would make a difference to a girl whose whole world was crumbling around her?

Chapter Thirty One- New Housemate

Amina, Asma and I now found ourselves with the problem of finding a house-mate to take up the fourth bedroom so that we didn't have to pay for it!

That was when Simone came in. She came up with the perfect solution when I told her about our predicament at Pop Mobility.

"You know Dani. I know someone who's unhappy in her shared house and wants to move. She's a lovely girl. I have a feeling you're going to like her."

Simone was right. There was nothing not to like about Carys. She was lovely. She came around to see our house the next weekend and had a good look around.

"What do you think?" I asked.

Carys nodded her head in approval.

"It's just right for me. When can I move in?"

Amina and Asma were of the same mind as me. We all liked this gentle, softly-spoken girl and so it was settled. Carys moved in the following weekend and the house was full again.

Our initial instincts about Carys were right. Carys turned out to be a decent housemate, careful and considerate of other people's needs, totally trustworthy. She always stuck to the rota and never needed to be reminded when it was her turn to do the cleaning.

She was always cheerful but underneath that outer cheer was an air of sadness about her. Sometimes, when she thought no one was looking, I would catch her sighing heavily, a deep, doleful sadness in her beautiful, wide, hazel eyes.

Carys was a beautiful girl though not in the conventional sense. Being of mixed heritage, she had her own look and it was beautiful. Golden brown skin, a heart-shaped face that tapered to a point, deep soulful brown eyes with long lashes and a slightly upturned nose made her a beauty, albeit one who had a tragic look about her sometimes.

It puzzled me why someone so young and so beautiful would have such a tragic air about her, why I would catch her sometimes looking so sad.

I didn't understand until the day I caught her crying when she thought she was all alone in the house.

All of us had gone out to campus and had been planning to stay on campus all day but my afternoon lecture had been cancelled unexpectedly so I came home early on the bus instead of being driven home by Asma in tow with Amina.

As I tiptoed gently up the stairs, I heard what sounded like a sob. Startled, I froze on the stairs. Then, I heard it again, another sob. It was coming from upstairs from the room that used to belong to Sophie and that now, belonged to our new house-mate, Carys.

My mind was in turmoil. What should I do? Should I feign ignorance, tip-toe to my room and pretend I hadn't noticed anything and leave her to cry alone or should I knock on the door, ask what's wrong and offer her comfort?

I remembered how Lara had confronted me when I was upset in the first year, how she had comforted me while I cried. I remembered how she had knelt in front of me and gently rubbed my back and spoken to me gently while I wiped away my tears.

Lara had taught me how to comfort people in distress. Thanks to her, I didn't tiptoe away out of embarrassment, unsure of what to do and how to behave.

Bravely, I walked up the rest of the stairs and knocked gently on Carys' door.

There was a silence, a slight rustling and then, Carys popped her head around the door, her face red, her eyes, puffy.

I must have looked concerned because when I asked,

"Carys, are you OK?" she shook her head.

"Can I help? Would it help to talk? I'm here if you need to talk."

She shook her head and sighed a deep sigh.

"No, I'm OK. Thanks," was her stoic response as she swallowed back tears and stifled a sob.

"Carys, you're not OK. You look as if you need a friend. It helps to talk sometimes. How about I bring us up a couple of mugs of hot tea and we talk about it? Everything feels better over a cuppa. We're housemates. We should look out for each other. Let me go down and get us both a cup of tea and we can talk it over, whatever's bothering you. You shouldn't be going through whatever you're going through alone."

Carys looked unsure but I gave her my most warm, reassuring smile.

She sighed as she sniffed, then reached back for a tissue from a box of tissues on her bedside table and blew her nose.

"Oh...OK. Thanks, Danita."

"Right. Five minutes. Give me five and I'll be back up with a cuppa for me and for you and you can tell me all about it. You look like you need some support."

It was just as well that Carys agreed to open up that day and accept support because that was the day I really got to know Carys. It was the day I got to know her story.

Chapter Thirty Two- Carys

October 1989, a beautiful girl of mixed heritage is in a communal room in a university hall of residence. One of sixteen teenagers all embarking on university courses, she appears nervous like many of the students around her in their first week away from home.

A boy sits across from the girl. He has a lean, smouldering, rebellious look about him like a modern-day James Dean, a rebel without a cause. His eyes are fixed on the nervous-looking girl who is seated opposite him. With her golden-brown skin, her wide, expressive hazel eyes, her dainty up-turned nose and her heart-shaped face that tapers to a perfect point, she is a beauty but she doesn't seem to know it.

The boy hones in on the nervous girl. His stare focuses mainly on her.

The girl shifts uncomfortably under the boy's intense stare but he is undeterred.

"So, you mean, he chased you?" I asked Carys as she went back in time to recount her story of how she and Stuart first met.

"Yes, he kept staring at me all the time. It was embarrassing. Every time I'd step into that kitchen, there he'd be with his laser eyes, looking right through me."

"Creepy," I said

Carys sighed.

"Well, no. I mean it was and it wasn't. I know it sounds really shallow but he was really gorgeous you know?"

"So are you!"

"I don't know. I don't feel it. I was bowled over that this really gorgeous guy liked me, you know? He made me feel like I was the most fascinating person in the world. No one has ever shown me that kind of attention, you know? I was always a bit of a drudge at home, looking after a sick parent and my little sister. I was always too busy being the sensible, responsible child carer to think about myself. I never really felt beautiful."

"Well, you are," I insisted.

"I was a bit on the plump side before my growth spurt so that affected my confidence as well."

"But you're not now. All kids have a bit of puppy fat. That's nothing unusual."

"So how come you were a child carer?"

"My parents divorced. He moved on, had another family and that left me, my baby sister Chantelle and my mum on our own. They both needed looking after. When she got sick, I had to be the sensible one, the carer because my sister's four years younger."

"My parents are divorced too but I'm an only child. There's only my mum and me in my household so we've got something in common."

"No brothers or sisters?"

"Nope. I begged Mum for one when I was a kid but I never got one. So, I lowered my sights. I asked for a cat but I never got one of those either. In the end, I settled for a ladybird!"

"A ladybird?"

"I know. I've had a tragic life."

Carys laughed at this and said,

"And I thought I had a sad life!"

"Well, there's always someone worse off somewhere," I replied "Like me with my ladybird. At least, you got a baby sister."

"Yeah. She really looks up to me. That's another pressure. I feel like I have set an example for her. She's fourteen now and looking after Mum like I did. We both had to grow up fast."

"I know. Most kids in single parent homes do but what upset you so much that you had to leave your student house mid-year?"

"Stuart. Stuart happened. He made me feel as if he couldn't live without me, as if I was special, the only girl in the world. He put me on a pedestal, and made me feel like he worshipped me. It's a big ego trip. It can be addictive when they do that you know.

So, here I am, always the carer, always the drudge, the carrier of burdens and suddenly, there's someone who's telling me that I'm beautiful, that I'm special, that they can't live without me because I'm so special. It's addictive, you know. Then, just when you give them your trust and they get what they want, they don't want it anymore and you realise that you've fallen prey to a manipulator."

"And that's what happened to you?"

Carys looked at me with that tragic look in her eyes and sighed deeply.

"Yes."

"It sounds to me as if he love-bombed you and then, let you down when he'd got what he wanted."

"He persuaded me that he loved me and I fell for it. He wore me down, making me feel that I was the only girl in the world. I didn't want to sleep with him because my mum got pregnant with me at nineteen but he said we could use birth control. He kept going on and on and on about it, pressured me, emotionally blackmailed me, said I didn't love him when I said I wanted to wait and eventually, he wore me down."

"And?"

"I cracked. I gave in to pressure. He swore that he loved me and wanted to spend the rest of his life with me."

Carys sighed, wiping away a tear that was glistening on her cheek.

I shook my head. I had a feeling I knew what was coming next.

"Once he got what he wanted, he started to be less attentive. He grew colder and more distant over time. I began to realise that he wasn't into me. He was into the thrill of the conquest. I felt like such a fool. He'd persuaded me to live with him in the second year. He couldn't do enough for me in the first year but after a year and a half, after I'd built my whole life around him, he started to take me for granted like I was part of the furniture. Then, one day, he said he needed some space, that it wasn't me. It was him. I asked him if there was someone else and he swore there wasn't and I believed him until I saw him with HER, holding hands."

"Bastard."

"I know. I felt such a fool."

"Was he your first?"

"Yes, and I wish he wasn't. I wish I'd waited now. I feel so used."

"I'm sorry hun," I reached forward sympathetically and squeezed her hand, gently.

Carys sighed deeply.

"Well, you live and learn. You won't be making THAT mistake again!"

"No way!"

"Can I give you another hug?"

Carys smiled and leaned forward so I could give her a hug. I had a feeling it was much needed.

That night, moved by Carys's story, I wrote a poem just for her. I named it ICE MAN and it went like this...

Ice Man

"It's over"

You told me coldly

In a tone that could shatter ice,

"I should have known it would be,"

I replied,

"Though it has been rather nice.

I should have known it would be,"

I muttered

Into my Bucks Fizz

"I always knew it would be
Everything always is."

"Yes, everything and always,"
You said,
With that strange, contemplative grin,

"Absolute concepts in a temporal world
Where time will always win

Where nothing is forever
Where ties are often severed
Where happy endings can never be
Because of our mortality

Sands can shift
Hearts can change
Wouldn't you agree?"

I looked into your tense, bright eyes
Flashed my most magnetic grin
"Of course," I said

You relaxed

You smiled

"Of course, you're right.

You win."

"Well, time to go"

Glance at your watch

Time to catch that train

Put out your ciggie

Down that Scotch

And head out

In the rain.

"Yes, it has been good

We must keep in touch

It has been rather... nice,"

Then, you catch your train

I fill my glass

ANOTHER – BLOCK - OF- ICE.

Chapter Thirty Three- Birthday Girl

As time went on, Carys settled in with us and began to come out of her shell. In the first year, her relationship with Stuart had consumed much of her time and she hadn't made many female friends. That all changed when she moved in with us.

I kept in regular contact with my friends from the year before. I saw them every day in lectures and seminars but now, I had a new set of friends in my house-mates and we began to form routines that gave us a sense of structure and stability. Every Sunday, we'd take turns to cook a home-cooked meal that we'd share.

When it was time for my birthday, I made my mother's korma, her own unique special recipe that had been passed down from mother to daughter. As we were all seated around the dining table, sharing my home cooked meal, we heard a chorus of voices singing under the open window.

"Happy birthday to you

Happy birthday to you

Happy birthday dear Danita

Happy birthday to you!"

I rose from my seat at the table and rushed over to the window. Looking out through the window, I could see the upturned, smiling faces of old friends from the year before.

"Come on up!" I yelled down to them through the open window. "You're just in time for Sunday lunch!"

And so, my old friends and my new friends all ended up sitting around the dining table together, tucking into my mum's pilau rice and chicken korma followed by mugs of tea and slices of birthday cake.

From this day forward, I was a teenage girl no longer. I had made it to becoming a woman in her twenties. Although I still felt like an awkward and diffident teenager sometimes, I was facing life as a grown-up and moving forward into the future.

Chapter Thirty Four- Electric Dreams

They say that "time flies when you're having fun." Well, student life must have been fun because before we knew it, we had entered into our third and final year and Carys, Emma and I found ourselves living back on campus in the same hall of residence after making a pact the year earlier to get back onto campus in the third year.

Now, as the end of our courses drew ever nearer, we were having to face the fact that our Halcyon days were not going to last forever and that this was coming to an end within a year.

Every year, when the final year students leave, they play Electric Dreams in the students' union as realisation sinks in that they're leaving the friends that they have made behind.

"We'll always be together

However far it seems

We'll always be together

Together in electric dreams."

So now, in our final year, Rob, who was doing English and Media Studies, made a video of all of us together to the tune of Electric Dreams!

There was Emma in a shopping trolley being carted around by her boyfriend Bryan. There was footage of Craig, traipsing around campus with a traffic cone on his head, looking a little worse for the wear after a Friday night pub crawl and there was footage of all of us at Alton Towers wearing 3D glasses at the 3D cinema, trying to catch non-existent balls as they flew at us from the 3D cinema screen!

It was hard to face the fact that in less than a year's time, these days of youthful exuberance days were coming to an end and we'd all have to go our separate ways and possibly, never see each other again.

Rob and Craig were still best friends despite their different personalities. Craig was cynical, sharp and edgy. Those sharp, dark, eagle eyes of his never missed a detail while Rob was a dreamer with a baby face, corn-coloured hair and dreamy forget-me-not blue eyes.

It's hard to believe that it had been two years since Craig had stuck a sanitary disposal bag on Rob's door and written "sick bag," on it and I had thought that Rob had put it there because he hated all women!

It seemed that Craig had been up to his old tricks again. Rob apparently got a dubious message sent to him on Valentine's Day. Someone sent him a card signed by an anonymous admirer with a silly poem that went something like this:

"Oh Robin Martin

You little sin bin

Such merry music you make

With your colossal ding-a-ling

Let us together make love, not war

Philosophically speaking

One can only say, "FWOARGH!"

It didn't take long for Rob to figure out the identity of his "anonymous admirer," because only someone close to him could know that his favourite mug that he drinks his tea out all of the time says, "Make Love, not war," as does his favourite T-shirt.

In the end, it turned out that Craig had done it to cheer Rob up after some kind of issue with his girlfriend, Anneliese. Rob was moping around the place after splitting up from his girlfriend, Anneliese. He wouldn't say why.

While Rob's romantic fortunes seemed to be on the decline, something was happening to Carys that was unexpected.

Now that we were back on campus, living in the same hall of residence, she had met a new man, a mature student of twenty-five. He was the same age as Paul, our pop mobility instructor, the one I had nearly skipped around in a circle with, back in the first year!

Both Carys and Donal are on the same Social Studies course but while they had seen each other in lectures, they only began speaking to each other when they found themselves in the same hall of residence in the third year. Their shared interest in Sociology, Social Studies and humanitarian work brought them close together after they had started chatting in the Communal kitchen every evening while making dinner.

Pretty soon, a bond began to develop between the two based on their shared interests and passions rather than on the smouldering physical attraction that there had been in the first year between her and Stuart. This time, it was love and not lust. There was no pressure, no emotional blackmail because like Carys, Donal was a do-gooder with a gentle heart who put the needs of others before his own.

Two do-gooders with the same passions and same goals had found each other after being hurt by others and I would often see them sitting over the dining table, their heads bent over an assignment, making each other cups of tea or coffee while studying quietly in the communal dining room.

Theirs was a quiet kind of love that was peaceful with no drama, a quiet love that grew organically between two selfless souls, each putting the needs of the other first. My heart filled with joy for my tragic friend Carys who for the first time in her life was settled and stable, and having unexpectedly found true love, was tragic no more.

Chapter Thirty Five- Rob

It was in the first term of the third year when it happened, the unthinkable. Lara was the one who told me. I had just entered the lecture room at noon when I spotted her waving furiously at me, beckoning me over.

Now that we were in the third year, we were back on campus but she was in a different hall of residence to me so it was the first time that day that I had seen her.

Unlike her usual poised self, she looked flustered as I made my way to join her.

"Have you heard the news about Robin, Dani?"

"What news?"

Lara took a deep breath and sighed.

"I don't know how to tell you this but Rob's in hospital. They think he could be dying."

"WHAAAT?" I yelled, losing all sense of time and place until I noticed the looks on the faces of other students around me. I slid down, embarrassedly, into the seat next to Lara.

"It's bad."

"What happened?"

"An overdose apparently. Craig found him lying lifeless on his bed, pills scattered around him. He's been rushed to hospital."

"Rob? An overdose? He's always so cheerful and happy. Why would Rob try and take his own life? Rob?"

"No idea. You never know what people are going through. Just because they're smiling on the outside doesn't mean that they're smiling on the inside."

"I know. I know," I said, remembering all the times I had put a brave face on things and had smiled even as a child when my whole world felt as if it was falling apart. If there was anyone who knew about the tears of a clown, it was me.

"Can... can we go and see him at the hospital?"

"His family, his mother and his brother are with him now and Craig. I'll try and find out what's going on. I have Craig's number. You can call him too if you like."

Lara ripped a piece of paper out of her diary and scribbled a number on it before handing it to me just before the lecturer stepped into the room and the lecture began...

That night, I gave Craig a call and asked him how Rob was doing. I asked for the name of the hospital and the ward and I asked if his family would mind if friends visited.

Craig sounded different to the Craig we all knew and loved. Gone was the jokey clown who liked to play pranks and tease everyone and in his place was someone bitter who kept snapping irritably at me down the phone. It was awkward. I didn't know what to say so I said,

"I'm so sorry Craig. We're all here for you if you need us. Rob's in everyone's thoughts and prayers."

"My nan told me she was praying for Rob. She even asked ME to pray," he said bitterly. "Pray? To what? To a non-existent sky fairy who doesn't exist except in wishful people's overactive imaginations. Pray and end up disappointed? No thanks! If there is a god in heaven, why would this happen to someone like Rob? Why are there so many innocent people in the world who suffer things they never deserved?"

I felt flustered in the face of such bitterness, such rage.

"I'm sorry. I'm sorry Craig. I don't know what to say. Bad things happen to good people. I know that. But without faith, I don't know how to cope. I have to hope and pray for a miracle when things happen. I don't know how else to cope."

Craig sniffed on the other side of the phone. I think he had been crying. And then, he said with an edge to his voice,

"There are no miracles Danita, no miracles for all the kids in the world who are being abused, for the women who are battered, for the men who die in unnecessary wars. There are no miracles because there is NO God!"

And then, he slammed the phone down.

It was awful.

I know that terrible things happen in the world all the time but I suspect that there is something more to this world than meets the eye because in my mother's family, there have been stories of premonitions coming to pass. I grew up with these stories. Some of my mother's people were like the people in the Bible.

One of the stories my mother told me was about her baby sister Ginny. My mum said that she was a lot like me. She was born in June and she was a chatterbox as a three-year-old just as I used to be when I was a little girl.

Mum said that my Aunty Ginny used to point to a spot in one of the rooms of their house where there was a bed on which my grandad used to sleep and she used to keep saying in her native Bengali,

"A little girl died here! A little girl died here!"

And she used to ask my granny obsessively for a white dress.

She was the little girl who, one day, suddenly collapsed and died on that spot, cradled in my grandfather's arms and they buried her in the white dress because the dead are buried in white in India and everyone wears white to the funeral.

Then, there was my mother's uncle who announced when he was eighteen,

"I dreamt that I died last night and you were all carrying my dead body to be buried."

Everyone laughed at him because he was so young until he died a few months later just as he had predicted. No one was laughing then when they carried his dead body to be buried at the funeral.

Things like this have happened so many times in my mother's family that are like something out of the scriptures of the world's great religions, it makes me suspect that there might be something more to this life than meets the eye, that there is a mystery behind all the suffering and all the pain.

What if God exists and what if we're in exile from him for some reason? What if the Biblical story is a parable? Jesus loved to teach in parables, the parable of the Prodigal Son and the father with the vineyard where the father and sons are not a real father with his sons but point to a greater reality where the father represents the creator and the sons represent the human race.

What if Adam and Eve stand for the entire human race, all men and all women?

What if the story about the snake is figurative, telling us that we betrayed God in some way as a race on the lies of an enemy and were sent down here for our loyalty to be tested until God lets us back into his circle of trust again?

If there isn't more to life than meets the eye, then why did my mother's relatives have premonitions come to pass all those times?

I suspect there is more to life than meets the eye. I would rather be on the safe side and believe than not believe and then, find myself in trouble on the other side.

Besides my mother's tales of the recurring premonitions in her family, Asma told me that the reason she's so devout at such a young age is because she used to suffer night terrors. She said she used to feel something pinning her down in her bed at night and sitting on her. She said that she was terrified but that praying daily made the terrifying attacks go away. That's why she is the way she is at such a young age.

Amina told me that a woman involved in the occult had testified that her rituals didn't work on people of one of the three Abrahamic faiths. She said that a higher power seemed to be protecting them.

In my religion, we're told that God sometimes hides himself from his creation to see what people will do if they think he isn't real if they think that they can get away with it. He wants to see their true colours. He wants to see what they do with the free will he has given them so he can give them exactly what they deserve on the judgement day.

I really love the song Woodstock that came out the year before I was born that goes:

We are stardust

We are golden

And we've got to get ourselves back to the garden."

What if we're in exile from God because we did something wrong and we have to pass tests before God trusts us and lets us back into the garden, into his circle of trust again?

So, I decided to err on the side of caution and to believe in a higher power. I decided to pray for Rob no matter what Craig said.

Chapter Thirty Six- Craig's Letters

Dear Nan

Thanks for your support and for your offer to come over. There's no need. I don't want you spending money from your pension to come over and support me. I can cope. I'm sorry I was off with you on the phone the other day.

I just don't have the belief you have in a higher power that loves everyone when I see all the horror in the world.

I love you Nan. Don't get me wrong and I respect your right to believe what you believe but I prefer to live in the real world and see it for what it is instead of comforting myself by telling myself fairy tales about a happy place where everyone is happy and nothing goes wrong when there's no proof that it exists.

I want to live my life being honest with myself about what's real instead of cushioning reality with comforting fairy tales, with a belief in a non-existent "father figure" in the sky who's going to make everything all right.

Remember when I was a kid Nan and you used to tell me about Santa and then, I found out he wasn't real? Well, how is God different to Santa? I grew up and realised that he didn't exist either!

I'm sorry I snapped at you when you called the other day. I know you meant well. I'm sorry. You've had a lot to put up with and you've never given up on me.

You stood by me the time I got fined for changing the sign on Stan's Dry Cleaners to Satan's dry cleaners after I got pissed with my mates after a few too many bevvies!

You stood by me when I changed the sign on the School of Arts to School of Farts with my mates when I was a kid!

You've always had your hands full with me Nan. You've always loved me. You've never given up on me.

I'm just worried about my little mate, Rob. Unlike you, I don't believe in a loving sky fairy who's going to make everything all right so I'm worried sick that he might die. Rob's so sensitive. He's such a dreamer. He's got no defences against the world. I was always worried he wouldn't make it, that the world would be too rough on him, that he wouldn't survive.

If you find praying helps, I'm happy for you Nan but it's not for me. I don't want to give myself false hope by believing in a non-existent sky daddy I can't be sure exists because there's no proof he does. Religion is just a drug for the masses, a reason to fight, a way to keep control.

I can't know that God exists but I do know that you do and that you're the one person in my life who's ever really loved me.

Thanks for everything Nan. Sorry again for snapping at you the other day.

Lots of love from

Your Craig.

Dear Greg

Still no news about Rob. I'm worried. There's a chance that we could lose him. People have been rallying around and offering their best wishes and some have even been passing on condolences as if he's already dead!

The other day, one of my ex-hall mates rang to ask about Rob. I was doing all right until she started going on about miracles and praying to God!

You know how these God-botherers wind me up. The last thing I need when my best friend is dying is a f....ing fairy tale!

I lost it at that point. I put the phone down.

I don't know how I'm going to get through the finals if Rob doesn't pull through. He's my best mate apart from you.

I'm calling his mum tonight to see if there's been any improvement. I'll let you know when I know.

Take care mate.

Craig.

Chapter Thirty Seven- Relief

The next few weeks were tense for all of us. One of us was dying. At least, that's what we thought but with spring came renewed hope, a chance for new beginnings.

Craig stopped snapping at us when it transpired that Rob was fighting back and making a recovery that was a little short of a miracle.

From the time, Craig had got back to their shared student house to find Rob passed out and cold and had called for an ambulance, Rob had been making steady progress towards coming back to us.

His mother had left his baby brother Thomas with her sister Carol and had carried out a bedside vigil, stricken with fear that her eldest child was dying. Craig had been a great support to Susan, Rob's mother almost like a third son and she, in turn, had asked the hospital to give Craig access to Rob as if he was a member of their own family.

Over the weeks, Rob made a slow but steady journey back to health and eventually when he was well enough to confide in Craig, the facts behind his overdose became known to all of us through Craig.

It turned out that Rob had been incited by two girls, Katrina and Sonia. They didn't exactly urge him to take his own life but their actions had led him into depression which led to the overdose that could have killed him and why did they do it? Why? Because of jealousy.

It transpired that Katrina and Sonia had been jealous of Anneliese, the baby-faced, delicate Anneliese with the big wide translucent eyes and corn-floured hair that matched

Rob's. She was resented by these two girls because of the bond she had with Rob because apparently, they had the hots for him so they had set to work, trying to separate the two by slandering Anneliese and claiming that she had the hots for other boys on campus.

This was all a lie. The devious Sonia had set a trap for Anneliese asking,

"Anneliese, do you find you fancy lots of boys on campus because I do."

The gentle, sensitive Anneliese, had tried to be kind by saying a non-committal, *"Uh huh,"* to spare Sonia's feelings and Sonia had pounced on that. She had lied to Rob who was infatuated with Anneliese, that Anneliese fancied lots of boys on campus and had a roving eye, that she was not serious about Rob at all.

Sonia had lied to Rob, not realising how sensitive he was to depression having lost his father two years earlier to alcohol poisoning.

Having stirred the pot like Iago, the master manipulator of Othello, the two girls had left Rob devastated. Instead of getting his friends to check with Annie's real friends how she really felt, he had fallen into a deep depression and had overdosed on sleeping pills.

While on the surface, Rob was a happy person, putting on a happy face, teasing his baby brother, tickling him and sitting on him to annoy him, deep down he carried scars, the scars of seeing his once fun-loving and happy dad slipping away, being consumed by an addiction he could not control.

"So, Rob's like me and Carys, putting on a smile in public when he's been through horror."

"How many of us are out there?" I wondered who wore a smile in public because they wanted to blend in and didn't want to be pitied, who'd known trauma at an early age and who had learned to hide their pain.

Just when Rob had been grappling with the loss of his dad, in came Sonia and Katrina with their jealousy and envy and in trying to hurt Anneliese, they had torn him apart.

"I thought she was special," he had confided in Craig. "I thought she was the one. I thought she was REAL. I was wrong. I was so wrong."

It was only after the overdose and Anneliese was found sobbing on the phone distraught by her friends that word got out that it was all a hoax and by then, it was too late, or so we thought.

I went to visit Rob with Craig one day and when I saw him after all those weeks in hospital, I was shocked. Gone was the chubby cheeked, baby-faced Rob I'd known in the first year. Just two years later, in the first term of the third year, he looked thin and gaunt as if he hadn't been fed properly since he left his mum at home!

I went to see him in hospital once to take a card and good wishes but Craig was there almost every day after lectures, supporting Rob and his mum as if he was one of the family. It was then that I realised that under Craig's cynical and apparently nonchalant exterior, there was a beating heart. He was passionate about the people he loved and loyal to the core where they were concerned.

Just before I was about to leave on the day I visited, the boys started having the most ridiculous conversation that went like this.

Rob asked Craig, "So, how are my goldfish then? Have you been remembering to turn the filter on? I don't want them dying in a tank full of fish wee, poo and farts!"

"Fish don't fart!" exclaimed Craig.

"Of course they do. How do you know that they don't?"

"Cos they haven't got an arse!"

"Course they do! They poo! I've seen the fish poo floating in the tank. Where does the poo come out of if they haven't got an arse? That's why you need to put the filter on!"

"Well, they don't fart! I've never seen bubbles coming out anywhere other than a fish's mouth!"

"But have you been putting the filter on?"

"YES!" replied Craig, looking a little red in the face.

"Good because the last time I left my fish with my neighbour, they were all dead in the tank when I came back cos she'd forgotten to turn the filter on!"

"I've got to go," I said as I stood up to leave. "Rob, we've all been worried about you. It's not the same without you. Get well soon."

And as I left the hospital that day, I knew that Rob was on the mend. I could tell from the reassuring way that he and Craig were bickering again! Things were getting back to normal...

Chapter Thirty Eight- New Beginnings

Blue skies were becoming more frequent now as winter was gently pushed aside by spring. It was calming to feel the soft kiss of the sun and the tender caress of the spring breeze while strolling through campus again.

The chirping of the birds in the morning was accompanied by the appearance of blossom on the trees, apple blossom and blushing pink cherry blossom. The world seemed to be waking up from a deep sleep as golden daffodils began to open up and turn their faces boldly to the sun.

And as nature blossomed, so did love. Carys, my once tragic housemate, was tragic no more for she had fallen in love again and this time, with the right man.

Gone was the haunted look in her wide, wistful, warm, brown eyes. Gone was the air of sadness and in its place, was an air of hope, a quiet hope for peace and happiness and better days to come.

I first noticed the growing bond between Carys and a fellow Sociology student, Donal, when he had ended up living in the same halls of residence as us in the third year. Donal was a couple of years older than us, having been born in the summer of 1969 that Bryan Adams, the American singer loved to sing about. He'd taken a couple of years off to do voluntary work for a charity abroad before starting his first year at university at the ripe old age of twenty when we had come in straight from school, a load of eighteen-year-olds.

Although Carys had seen him about in Sociology lectures, they had never been in a seminar together and they only came into close contact with each other when they ended up living in the same hall of residence in the third year.

Their first meeting point was the communal kitchen where they pored over Sociology books while making cups of tea and coffee for each other and discussing the latest assignment for their course.

Theirs was a gentle kind of love that grew organically over time with no pressure put on one by the other. Both Carys and Donal were the eldest child in their families, sensible and responsible and used to taking care of others. Two selfless and kind people had found each other, two do-gooders with no ego who would spend their lives putting each other first. There would be no rows in their home, no spats, no fights because they were both such gentle, sweet souls.

Looking at them, I wondered whether I would ever be lucky enough to find true love. Lara had scared me off Daniel talking about free love and LSD and the sixties. Then, there was Mrs Harding talking about Liquorice All Sorts and my mother warning me that I had to put God first and be perfect because I was a child of divorce, a child without a father who couldn't make any mistakes because, I didn't have a wealthy father to put things right for me if I did.

With all this pressure on me to be perfect, I had never known what it was to be young and carefree so when my joyous, happy, bubbly friend from a happy home had optimistically chosen Top of the World as her favourite Carpenters song, I had chosen Goodbye to Love at just eighteen years old.

"I'll say goodbye to love

No one ever cared if I should live or die

Time and time again

The chance for love has passed me by

And all I know of love

Is how to live without it

I just can't seem to find it."

Where other women saw fairy-tale romances when a man approached them, I saw danger unless others told me it was safe to go forward. I had absolutely no confidence of my own.

Chapter Thirty Nine- Cog In A Machine

With Rob on the mend and reuniting with the lovely Anneliese and with my beautiful friends Carys and Donal finding true love, life seemed to be looking up and the first term of the third year passed without any further incidents.

Week after week, we attended lectures and seminars as usual and before we knew it, both the first and second terms of the third year were over and we found ourselves in the final term of the final year of our studies with final year exams looming over us, the outcome of which would determine our futures.

"It's all downhill from here," joked Craig one Friday afternoon when we had all congregated in our usual place up at the students' union.

"This is it, the end of our glory days. Not long now before we all go out into that mad, bad world and become just another cog in a corporate machine, leaving all our dreams behind us, just another number, another wage slave. It's all downhill from here," he re-iterated after he burped contentedly having downed his glass of cider.

I shifted uncomfortably in my seat, fiddling with my glass that I'd just emptied of blackcurrant juice and Cola.

"Is this really the end of our Halcyon days, safe in the bubble of academia? Is it really going to be all downhill from here?" I wondered worriedly. "I hope that's not true," I thought to myself and as I put down my empty glass on the table, I prayed quietly that Craig was wrong.

Chapter Forty- Finals

Before long, we found ourselves in the final term of the final year with exams approaching fast on the horizon. It was time to go into hermit mode and start revising for the exams that were going to determine my future.

I had read dozens of books on my literature course and I knew that over time, I'd probably remember only a few out of the hundred that I had read, the really good ones.

Apart from the classic English favourites of Pride and Prejudice, Sense and Sensibility and Emma written by our own tragic Jane Austen and the gems left by the equally tragic Bronte sisters such as Jane Eyre, The Tenant of Wildfell Hall, Wuthering Heights, etc, I had also come to appreciate some works of American literature that were just as good.

Who could forget Edith Wharton's portrayal in The House of Mirth of the unfortunate Lily Bart, a naïve girl, a victim of cultural conditioning and hypocrites in society who projected their own failings onto her and scapegoated her for their own sins, leading to her tragic, untimely demise. Lily reminded me of the girl in the Cat Steven's song, Wild World, someone ill-equipped to deal with the real world, someone like Rob. How we loved him for his sensitivity, his innocence but those were the very things that had nearly killed him in this wild world full of false people who project their own failings onto others and cause their deaths.

Then, there was the award-winning American author, Ralph Ellison who named his novel Invisible Man to show his protagonist's frustration with social prejudices that leave him feeling that he is invisible, that no one sees him for who he truly is as an individual because they are too busy stereotyping him for the colour of his skin. Even a man of his own colour, Bledsoe sees him as competition and a threat and tries to jealously tear him down! So how does the protagonist cope in a world in which no one sees him for who he truly is because of all the villains he faces of other colours and even his own?

It was no wonder that Ellison won an award for his portrayal of the struggle of the sensitive and idealistic individual in a world where he did not fit in and where everyone, even his own people, gathered to tear him down!

Yet, another novel that had made an impression was Upton Sinclair's, The Jungle in which a young couple, Oona and Jurgis, leave their countryside home to seek the American dream only to find it an urban nightmare.

These powerful novels about the struggles of the underdog, the less fortunate, the minority, and the single female were stories that touched my heart because like Donal and Carys, I was a do-gooder and I used my own wounds not to seek sympathy and pity from others but to learn empathy and work to make a world that was fairer so that the Oonas and the Jurgises of the future didn't suffer.

I knew I would carry Oona, Jurgis and the Invisible Man in my heart for a long time to come and in exams, I would have to write about them among other things I had learned.

At twenty years of age, I was still a girl-woman and not yet the mature woman my mother was with her culinary expertise. Despite her constant reminders in letters to eat home-cooked food, at twenty, I still hadn't blossomed into the sensible, domestic guru that my mother had become over the years.

My diet consisted of easy-to-make meals of baked potatoes with beans, toast with beans or Toast Toppas, ocean burgers and chips sold up at the students' union or runny vegetarian soup dispensed from the soup machines with tiny bits of green or carrot floating amid the runny, hot, flavoured water!

On one occasion, when exhausted by revision, I stood beside a soup machine, wailing,

"Oh no! Oh no! Oh noooo!!!" as I watched my soup go down the machine vent because there was no cup to receive it! All the paper cups had run out that day.

On another occasion, I swore a life-long aversion to potatoes after having one too many baked potatoes! I swore I never wanted to eat another potato again as long as I lived! I was sick of potatoes.

Despite this teenage girl diet, I somehow managed to get through the four final exams at the end of the year and then, slept for hours, trying to recover, one day, waking up at 5pm from a long, deep slumber! We were all worn out after finals and then, there was the anti-climax after exams while we waited for the results to be announced because impoverished student that I was, I had no money to go anywhere or to do anything much to celebrate!

So, once exams were over, there was a period of waiting with friends to see whether we had all passed our exams on the all-important judgement day – exam results day!

Chapter Forty One- Results

Finally, it dawned, the day that we had all been waiting for.

I groaned as I woke up that morning and peered out at the clock from beneath my bed cover. It was time to get up, time to face the truth. The culmination of two years' work (the second and third year of my three-year course) would be displayed on one of the many exam noticeboards.

I had made plans to meet Emma and Lara by the noticeboards outside the Humanities building around 11 am as all three of us had been studying for English degrees. I had been reading English and American Literature. Lara had been reading English and European Literature and Emma had been reading English with Education as she planned to be a primary school teacher like her mother when she went back to Wiltshire.

So, as I headed for the exam boards, I wasn't surprised to see a sparkling-eyed, rosy-cheeked, bouncy Emma bounding over to me excitedly.

"So, Danikins, are you ready?"

I shook my head.

"I'll never be ready so I might as well just go and get it over with," I replied, my heart, doing somersaults in my chest.

"Over here!" Lara was already by the boards and gesturing for us to join her. There was a big smile on her face.

"I take it she's already looked at the exam boards and knows she's done well," Emma observed as we walked on up to join Lara.

"Did you get the 2:1 you wanted Lara?" I asked as I reached her.

"Yes. I did. Thank God!" she beamed at me.

"Well done!" Emma and I said in unison as Lara encouraged us to move forward.

I edged slowly forward, craning my neck to see my name and my grade. Finally, I managed to get to the front and there I saw my name and my grade – Danita Khan, upper second.

A wave of relief swept over me. My three years at university had not been in vain. All that hard work in the last few weeks had not gone down a drain, unlike my ill-fated, watery, machine soup on exam day!

Looking to my left, I spotted Emma putting her hand to her chest in a gesture of relief as she found her result on her part of the board. We had all got 2:1s and poverty or not, the next night, Friday night was going to be a time for celebration as we all gathered in the students' union for the last time.

Every year since the first year, they had played Electric Dreams in the student union for the final year students who were leaving the next morning and they'd all sing in unison to the words,

"We'll always be together

However far it seems

We'll always be together

Together in electric dreams."

And at that instant while we were all singing together, I could just imagine Rob, our English and Media friend, doing a film sequence of us in slow motion of our happiest times together over the years, the water fights in the summer when we turned up to lectures dripping wet, the jelly fight in the first year with jelly ending up on Andy's bum, the pranks we played in Rag Week to raise money for charity, the silliness, the teenage high jinks and the days spent lying on the summer grass looking up at the blue, blue summer sky or playing Frisbee! I could imagine him setting it to the tune of "The Way We Were," the sentimental song that Barbara Streisand sang so well.

I wish he had filmed all those special moments because pretty soon, all this was going to be a memory...

The next morning as I bid my friends farewell, there was much hugging and crying and promises to keep in touch although we knew, deep in our heart of hearts, that things would never be the same.

"Keep in touch, Danita. You've got my number, haven't you?" asked Lara as she gave me a warm hug just as she did after the disagreement I had had with my mother back in the first year.

"I'll miss you Danikins!" Emma exclaimed as she enveloped me in a warm, bear hug and then, when she saw the tears glistening in my eyes, she added,

"It's not goodbye. It's au revoir Danikins. We'll keep in touch and there's still graduation day! We'll see each other on graduation day!!"

Chapter Forty Two – Graduation Day

A month after we left university, we were all going back to the old place one last time for graduation day. All new graduates had been issued with two tickets for guests and most people were taking their parents as the day their baby graduated was a proud day for the parents.

For people like me, the children of single parents, things were different. I took my mother and Dinah, a friend from school who I had known since I was twelve. Dinah was my father-substitute on graduation day!

Why Dinah? Because Dinah had been the recipient of my many letters home, gushing about Daniel, the boy with the "poetic and romantic hair," and the adorable upturned nose. Dinah was the one I had written to when he had sneezed in the lecture and I had been overwhelmed and moved deeply enough by the beauty of his sneezes to pen a poem celebrating them! "The Lady Writes An Ode Upon Her Lover's Nose," had been written when we were studying the Courtly Love Tradition which included poems about pale lovers loitering about lakes, La Belle Dame Sans Merci and so on.

Dinah had been the one I had written to when I had fled a seminar in a fit of giggles which I disguised as a coughing fit when the lecturer had said something that sounded like a rude word!

Every year, for three years, I had been writing home to Dinah about the boy I had adored from afar, from a safe distance, and at last, she was going to see him in the flesh, the boy I had been raving about on graduation day!

"His name is Daniel, Daniel Davis. You will remember, won't you Dinah?"

I had nagged her again and again to remember his name until she had wanted to strangle me!

But when graduation day finally dawned, searching the sea of faces before me in the auditorium, there was one face that was missing- the face of the boy with the "Poetic and romantic hair."

"He's not here!" I complained to Dinah. "This was my last chance to see him and he's not here!"

Dinah sighed in commiseration and I was crushed. I had searched for him at the last night disco when they had played Electric Dreams but to no avail. He wasn't there and he wasn't here either! I had counted on seeing him for one last time on graduation. Surely, he wasn't missing the all-important graduation day as well?

But then, at the last minute, who should slide into the empty seat in the row in front of me but Daniel? He had made it just in time before the ceremony was about to begin! I sighed a sigh of deep relief as he slid down into his seat.

Each of us had been given a booklet with the names and grades of all those who were graduating on the same day as us. Given the large numbers of Humanities students graduating, we had to wait patiently for our names to be read out one by one so that each graduate could mount the podium, shake the hand of the master of ceremonies and be handed a scroll with which they would later be photographed. The degree certificate itself would arrive in the post later.

We sat and waited patiently as one by one, the new graduates walked onto the podium. It felt like endless waiting but there were some moments of laughter along the way like when the master of ceremonies read out the name

Susan Beryl. I had to stifle a laugh and I could see Daniel's shoulders shaking as he did the same! That poor girl Susan had a middle name that was a granny name like Charlene in the hit Australian TV soap Neighbours.

My generation had laughed when Scott Robinson from Neighbours found out at the altar that he was marrying an Edna much to Charlene's embarrassment. She was a Charlene Edna and here was another girl with much the same predicament. She too had been named after her nan!

Talking of nans, I had spotted Craig earlier with his nan. He'd given us a cheery wave. I could see from the protective arm he had around her that the boy loved his nan. She looked a bit like Mrs Harding, my neighbour from my early years in Stockwell who used to knit me jumpers and buy me encyclopaedias when I did well at school. She used to say, *"I'm your English granny!"* You've got to love your gran!

After the chuckle we had over the girl with the granny name, there was another faux pas when the master of ceremonies mispronounced an ethnic name. Everyone who watched the hit TV series Fame from the eighties when we were kids knew that Le Roy is pronounced Lee Roy and not Le Roy but apparently the master of ceremonies had never watched Fame and had never seen the character in the show leap across the dance studio in his tights and legwarmers so he pronounced the name awkwardly as Le ROY, causing more stifled merriment among the younger generation.

It felt like ages before our names were called and we all had to leave our seats to line up at the side of the podium. We filed out in our caps and gowns to shake hands with the master of the ceremonies and receive the scroll with which we would be photographed for our official graduation photo.

Once it was finally all over, as we all stepped out of the auditorium into the fresh summer air, one of the graduates started doing a victory dance and a finely dressed lady in a beige skirt suit with a straw hat said worriedly to her daughter, *"Poor boy seems to be having a fit,"* to which her daughter responded with slight scorn, *"He's dancing mother!"* The daughter then turned and smiled at me while rolling her eyes in exasperation as if to say, *"PARENTS!"* She happened to be Lara, my old friend who I had misunderstood in the early part of the first year but, who I now counted as one of my best friends, and I smiled back. I suppose dancing meant something different to our generation than theirs!

My mind travelled back to a night when my friends Lara, Emma and another girl called Clare had all been laughing about their dads dancing like dads! Lara said that her father did the exaggerated sidestep. Emma pitched in saying that her dad, a sports teacher, danced as if he was running a Marathon, and Clare had demonstrated how her dad danced as if he was about to punch someone! The conversation ended when they had all turned to me expectantly and found that I had nothing whatsoever to add to the conversation. I hadn't had a father since primary school and I had no idea if he ever danced or even liked dancing!

But WE had all danced together that night at the last night disco as we sang along to Electric Dreams, knowing it was the last time we would ever dance together and the last time that we would all be together as a group before graduation day.

Once the official graduation photographs had been taken, it was time to return the gowns. Immediately after the ceremony, I quizzed Dinah,

"Did you see him? Did you see him? Did you see Daniel? Did you take a picture?"

"Huh?" Dinah looked confused. "I thought you said he wasn't coming!"

Disappointment engulfed me; she hadn't seen him after all the letters I had sent home singing his praises and writing poems about his sneezes! I had hoped she'd take a photo of him as he strode onto the podium so that I would have a memento of the boy I had admired from afar at university but had never dared to speak to. I was the timid girl with the timid knock who never dared to speak to the forbidden fruit for fear of falling in love with it. I had never dared to break the rules because following the rules kept you safe, didn't it? At least, that was what I had been raised to believe.

So, when I went to return my robes and I saw Daniel, to say that I forgot myself and lost my composure would be an understatement. After years of repression and hiding how I felt about him, for one brief moment, I forgot to be dignified. I forgot to be poised. I forgot to be sensible.

"THERE - HE - IS!" I shouted at the top of my voice like an adoring fan who has just seen her favourite pop star!

I didn't just shout. I was pointing!

"WHERE? WHERE?" replied Dinah determined to get a good look at the boy she had heard so much about for the past three years in letter after letter and then, she STARED at him intensely to get a really good look at him!

At this point, I realised what I had done and how embarrassing I had been and to my horror, Dinah kept staring at him to the point that he started flapping the lapels of his jacket in embarrassment, literally flapping, turned a beetroot-red and then hung his head looking embarrassed.

I felt terrible. "What have I done?" I thought, biting my lip in embarrassment. "First, I ignore him for three years because of a promise I made to my mother before she let me go to university to never embarrass her by having a boyfriend and now, I embarrass him by squealing in delight at the sight of him and pointing like an over-excited child with no manners! On top of that, my friend from home is now STARING at him and he's looking overwhelmed as if he doesn't know what to do with himself! What have I done? Why am I such a fool! I am so embarrassed, behaving like an over-excited teenager at the age of twenty-one!"

And that was the last time I saw Daniel. That was how it ended, the relationship that had never begun.

In the end, my mother had triumphed. Her god had triumphed. Her fear of

"What will people say about the fatherless child of divorce if she has a boyfriend on top of all her disadvantages?" had triumphed and I was going home intact.

There had been, "no drinking, no smoking, no boyfriends and no pork." I had been a good girl and I had followed the rules. I had kept my promise to my mother.

What I was going to get for being a good girl still remained to be seen.

After returning the gowns, we called a cab to take me, my mother and Dinah back to the bed and breakfast where we were staying for one more day before heading back home on the coach, all three of us, to London, the city where I was born.

Yet, although London was the city where I was born, the happiest years of my life had been spent in the university town where I had been a student for three years, ensconced in a safe, academic bubble surrounded by like-minded people who had become my friends and neighbours, people who had begun to feel like family and then, just when I had got used to it all, it was all being taken away!

For three years, we had become one, one group, one people. On campus, we had all belonged together. Our ancestors had come from different parts of the globe, and for three years, at this campus university, we had all become one people. We had all belonged.

But now, the bubble was broken and we were each going our separate ways. We were all going home.

It wasn't long before the taxi arrived to take us away from campus back to the bed and breakfast. As I climbed into the taxi with my mother and Dinah, I turned around and took one long, last, lingering look at the place that had become home, the place that had been my home for the last three years and as I did, there were tears in my eyes, tears for the friends I had made, tears for Daniel who I would never see again and tears for the life that I was leaving behind..

So, it was goodbye to the world of water fights, jelly fights and schoolgirl pranks and hello to the world of adult responsibility, to the world of mortgages and bills, to the world of the rat race and the treadmill.

And as the driver put his foot firmly down on the accelerator and we pulled away from campus, I hoped to God that we would see each other again, that our friendships would never fade.

I hoped to God that Craig was wrong, that it was not going to be all downhill from here, the last of our glory days. I hoped for a brand, new beginning and I prayed to God in his heaven that it would NOT be the end.

Chapter Forty Three- Time Tells

As the strains of the hit song, Electric Dreams, float in through her office window, Dr Gloria Taylor looks down benignly on the graduates in their caps and gowns, milling about, flanked by family and friends on this, their special day, a day of jubilant celebration marking a successful end to three years of academic study before the young graduates make their way into the adult world.

After contemplating the scene serenely for some minutes from her office window, the professor turns her back to the window and seats herself squarely at her solid oak desk on which sits her diary, and she writes..

Every year, they come in droves, straight out of school, fresh-faced, starry-eyed, rosy-cheeked leaving friends and family behind to embark on a new adventure, three or four years of academic study in the safe bubble of academia before they leave to become participants in the real world beyond these hallowed halls.

And every year, another batch leaves, shedding tears, bidding fond farewells, making promises to keep in touch as they go their separate ways back to the bosom of the family and friends they left behind, back to the real world.

Will these youthful friendships last forever or will the world come between them and make strangers out of friends?

Only time will tell...

Printed in Great Britain
by Amazon

58280130R10108